# *Praise for*
# Giulio Mozzi

"I read Giulio Mozzi's first book with real enthusiasm. What struck me most was his everyday language. Even when his subjects rely on metaphor, his words are plain, and so turn mysterious."—Federico Fellini

"This writer has taken the floor with the tone of someone laying down the law."—Tiziano Scarpa

"There's no escaping this relentless prose."—Marco Lodoli

"Mozzi speaks of irretrievable loneliness, of the longing for love, but also of those violent impulses rising from the depths of the human heart, the shadows within."—Enzo Siciliano

"Gorgeously rooted in the best modernist tradition of writers like Italo Calvino and Antonio Tabucchi, Giulio Mozzi is among the most fiercely literary authors emerging from Italian literature today. . . . Elizabeth Harris's translation beautifully renders the noble grit of Mozzi's distinctive voice."—Minna Proctor

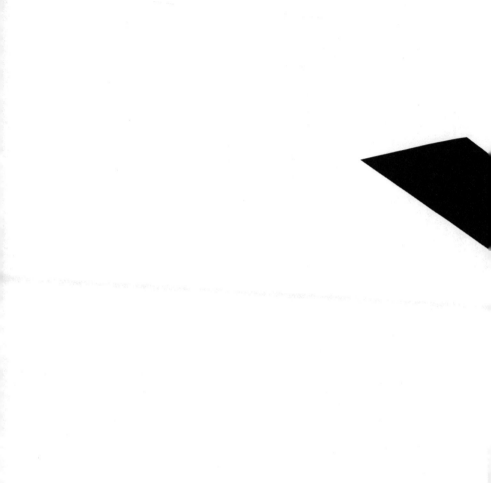

THIS IS THE GARDEN

Giulio Mozzi

Translated from the Italian by Elizabeth Harris

OPEN LETTER
LITERARY TRANSLATIONS FROM THE UNIVERSITY OF ROCHESTER

Copyright © 2005 Alpha Test S.r.l. – Sironi Editore, Italy
Translation copyright © 2013 by Elizabeth Harris
Originally published in Italy as *Questo è il giardino*

First edition, 2013
All rights reserved

Versions of these stories first appeared in the following journals: "The Apprentice,"
*AGNI Magazine*; "Glass," *AGNI Online*; "Cover Letter," *The Kenyon Review*; "On the
Publication of My First Book," *The Literary Review*; "F.," *The Massachusetts Review*;
"Claw," *The Missouri Review*; "Trains," *Two Lines Online*; "Tana," *Words Without Borders*.

Library of Congress Cataloging-in-Publication Data:

Mozzi, Giulio, 1960-
   [Questo e il giardino. English]
   This is the garden / by Giulio Mozzi ; Translated from the Italian by
Elizabeth Harris. — First Edition.
      pages cm.
   "Originally published in Italy as Questo e il giardino."
   ISBN-13: 978-1-934824-75-7 (pbk. : alk. paper)
   ISBN-10: 1-934824-75-5 (pbk. : alk. paper)
   I. Harris, Elizabeth (Translator) II. Title.
   PQ4873.O993Q4713 2014
   853'.914—dc23
                                    2013022493

This project is supported in part by an award from
the National Endowment for the Arts.

**ART WORKS.**
arts.gov

Printed on acid-free paper in the United States of America.

Text set in Minion, a serif typeface designed by Robert Slimbach in 1990 and
inspired by late Renaissance-era type.

*Design by N. J. Furl*

Open Letter is the University of Rochester's nonprofit, literary translation press:
Lattimore Hall 411, Box 270082, Rochester, NY 14627

www.openletterbooks.org

*This Book*

*This book would never have been written if Laura Pugno, my perfect friend, had not taught me to write. This book would never have been translated without the passionate dedication of Elizabeth Harris. My thanks, then, to Laura and Elizabeth.*

*And finally, I thank you as you hold this book in your hands and might read it.*

*—Giulio Mozzi*

# *Contents*

Questo è il giardino; se lo guardi è forte
il lume tanto che ti fere gli occhi
e ti rivolti, ma subito apprendi
che tutto è vero, ogni cosa che vedi
è vera, e svolge la vita nel tempo
e è intera . . .

This is the garden; when you look it's far
too bright and burns your eyes
and so you turn away, although you know
that everything is real, everything you see
is real, and through time life unwinds
and is complete . . .

—Claudio Damiani, from "Il giardino del mio amore"
("The Garden of My Love": Fraturno, Rome: Abete 1987)

# THIS IS THE GARDEN

# *Cover Letter*

Dear *Signorina*,

Please find enclosed your two letters (I imagine you recognized them right away), which I'm returning because I don't think it puts me at too much risk. I won't return your money—I spent most of it anyway on things I need—and I won't return your purse, which I destroyed, or the other things I found in your purse that I hope didn't hold too much practical or sentimental value. You must have gotten your ID cards by now: I tossed them in a mailbox like always (I know the mail is reliable). I'm afraid you've already changed your locks, and in a way I'm sorry about this, since there's no benefit for me and it was a waste of money for you, as your keys—along with everything else—wound up in a trash bin, where I'm fairly sure no one will fish them out, and even if someone did, without your address, he'd have no idea what to do with them. For security reasons, I generally don't save or resell what I find in a purse, even if it's worth something. But I always go through purses carefully—you never know—there might be some kind of medicine that a person has to carry at all times for a life-threatening illness like diabetes or heart disease. While I'm sure there'd be some risk, you should know: if I found this type of

3

medicine, even if it can be replaced at any pharmacy, I wouldn't think twice about returning it as quickly as possible, and that's why I've memorized the numbers for two express delivery services. Actually, so far I've only found aspirin, other headache remedies, eye drops, etc. I once kept a lottery ticket, but then I realized I'd never bought a lottery ticket in my life, and a sudden windfall—even a spectacular one— might not turn out to be such a happy event for me. You should never own something you didn't desire first, I thought, so I tossed the ticket.

I considered just sending back your two letters in a sealed envelope without any note at all—you might have appreciated the gesture, found it chivalrous or something, but you might also worry about this stranger who maybe read your personal letters and could even be dangerous. Sorry I'm letting myself imagine your thoughts, but since we can't meet, I don't have much choice. I even had your letters sealed in another envelope, but then I couldn't send it. I decided to add this note because I'm not returning the letters to be chivalrous (I don't even know what that word means, really), and I wouldn't feel right if you had some ideas about me that weren't true. I know this is a strange situation—believe me, I find it just as strange as you do. But you need to know that I have no plans to contact you further after this letter. I won't save your address; I won't sneak into your house; I won't make obscene phone calls in the middle of the night. I know some people who would, and that's why I'm giving you these examples. Please believe me: nothing like this has ever crossed my mind.

I'm in the odd position of having to keep our conversation going even though we can't meet and we can't talk. A conversation's only possible between two people who know and accept one another, who have a reciprocal relationship; in our case, this reciprocity must be set aside. I assure you I'm not happy about this, and if my letter is some type of written monologue, please understand I never wanted to keep you from answering; I'm just looking out for my personal safety.

From a strictly technical point of view, I also could have called; that probably wouldn't be too risky; but a phone call wouldn't work. As soon as I said, "I'm the one who stole your purse" (and something like that over the phone can only sound ugly), you'd have an immediate emotional reaction, and that would be the end of any normal conversation. No matter how you react to the first read-through, this letter will still be there, so you can read it a second time, after your head has cleared. Besides, I think a letter's the best method for saying what needs saying, and as clearly as possible: if you can revise, you can be more precise, more honest. But maybe since speech is more spontaneous, you think it's more honest. A lot of people do. I know plenty of businessmen who'd rather take an exhausting, expensive trip than close a deal without meeting the other party face-to-face. You've got to believe me—I'm being absolutely truthful here—I don't think a person can lie in writing: you can lie out loud, and what you say won't leave a trace; your words can mean one thing while your tone, your expression, can mean something else; but a piece of writing can be read over, mulled over, so I really don't think it's possible to insert lies without leaving some trace of evidence behind. What I mean is that in a letter, even if you want to tell the truth but can't, maybe you're too cautious or shy, there's an involuntary truth that seems to come out anyway that's impossible to avoid.

So I have to confess I spent some time reading your two letters, even if they weren't mine. I've never found letters in a purse before, and I had this vague notion that a letter, like someone's medicine, might hold some crucial piece of information, some address or recommendation. I'm not used to writing letters—it feels a bit awkward. Reading this, I can see I'm drawing a strange portrait of a thief as someone not exactly "honest" but "sensitive," anyway. I must admit I'm not at all interested in making the consequences of my thefts out to be more serious than they really are. I'll take responsibility for a theft, but in some ways I don't want to be held responsible (e.g., in front of a judge) for someone else's life. I don't want you to get the wrong idea about me, and perhaps that's making me too verbose; my apologies. I have to say that I'm not inclined to think of myself as a thief. I live this way because I want to, but if someone else chooses a different lifestyle, I don't hold it against him. There's plenty of wealth to go around in this world, and I don't think you can criticize someone if he limits himself to taking only what he needs. I don't like harming people more than I gain for myself. This is a good rule of caution—maybe it's the first rule of caution. I'm not some addict who just goes out and steals for a fix. I want you to understand this, even if it's also true that I consider a certain number of cigarettes a day to be something I need. Since you didn't have cigarettes or a lighter in your purse, you must not smoke, so what I consider a "need," you might not find all that convincing. I'll admit: I want to make a good impression.

I do a job a week—that's usually enough—so I can take my time. It's a modest living. You know how much money you had in your purse, and you have to trust me when I tell you that this is plenty for one week, even with the small amount I always set aside. I know people who think they live on next to nothing and spend the same amount in just two days—and unlike me, they don't even pay rent. I try to give money its due, and if deep down you object that I don't earn my money, consider this: I do get it at some personal risk. I'm extremely careful, I've never been caught, and I know if I pay close attention, I can reduce this risk, but I can't eliminate it entirely. I don't want you to romanticize me as some criminal character. I'm not in any criminal circles, I don't know any other working thieves, and most of all, I don't hang out with fences. But don't get the idea I look down on these people, either. I stay away to be safe. Fences and chronic thieves (people who steal because that's the only thing they know) almost always have records, and they all have to do a little informing, just to survive. I don't want a life that's always on the inside, on the outside . . . so if I want to keep living the way I live now, and I do, I have to stay as far as I can from this small, side world that I really don't know anyway, or I know it the way you know it, from what's in the papers. But I do have to admit, when I find myself with something gold in my hand, I'm awfully tempted.

A couple of years ago, I found a pamphlet under my door, probably slipped under there by some of the parish boys, about a project for digging wells in an extremely dry part of Central Africa. The pamphlet included an address, so about once a month, when I find something valuable (usually gold lighters, but sometimes pens or earrings), that's where I send it. Maybe this sounds ridiculous, but otherwise, I'd just toss this stuff out, which seems like a waste.

Truthfully, I'm not entirely sure what a thief *is*. If I happened to meet one, I'd never think of swapping trade secrets. It's not like we'd have some special bond just because we're both thieves. No, if I met a thief, I'd watch my wallet.

On the other hand—and this will sound strange—I do need to feel something for the ladies who (just between you and me) I like to call my clients. This word, it didn't come to me right away. There's a reason for stealing purses instead of wallets. It's easier. Young women are a bit more distracted than older women, and this little bit means a lot. I prefer "clients" to "victims," because when it comes down to it, I really don't think what I'm doing is all that bad. Stealing a purse is something you can't hurry; that would be reckless. On a Saturday afternoon, I'll go out for a walk like everyone else. I'll people-watch, window-shop. Most of the girls going into the department stores on Saturday carry a bit more money in their purses. And more than likely, they'll spend that money on something superfluous, or at least on something they want and don't need; so working in a department store on a Saturday, I'll get good results, and I also won't feel like I'm stealing anything that essential. In department stores, people wander around, and no one's surprised to see the same face two or three times. Everyone's happy just wasting time: it's normal for someone to set her purse down, to leave it for a few minutes on a counter, by a display, while she picks out something she likes, touches the fabric, inspects it for flaws, compares colors. I don't think it's particularly dangerous telling you all this—we have so many department stores here. But it's not safe, either, always working in the same city, so every once in a while, I'll take a trip.

So as I was saying, I need to like my clients. This probably has something to do with my sense of guilt (I was raised, as you probably were, to respect the rules), but liking my clients has its practical side, too. In a crowded place, no one's surprised to see some guy staring at a pretty girl—as long as he doesn't overdo it, of course. Sometimes I'll pick out a few small things I need, then find a sales counter with a long line so I can look around. No one remembers the guy standing next to her in line. If you don't mind my saying, you're very pretty, and I liked you right away.

It's easier to read someone you like. You can't just wait for her to leave her purse on a counter—she needs to do it two or three times so you can figure out how distracted she is, how long the distraction lasts, how intense it is (or maybe "un-intense" is better). Then you need to make sure no one's looking, that everything's close, you're in a good spot, the exit's clear and easy to reach. It takes a lot of patience. I like to see someone staring at everything, all the items for sale, then coming closer, staring at a group of things, focusing in on one, doing the math. I like seeing her concentration kick in (and it's during this concentration/distraction that I can make my move). There's little outward sign of her concentration, but it's very decisive, very intense. She devotes herself completely to the thing she's picked, and everything else, the room, the people, the noise of the store, they all disappear. I'm lost in the moment, too—but in secret. I have to admit I watched you more closely than normal: you're especially graceful and charming, and I decided to take a moment to enjoy, in spite of the risk. I'm lucky I enjoy my job of watching others so much; I look pretty natural doing it. With all the details I've brought up, it must seem like I'm writing a book; but I've never tried to describe what I do before, it feels a little strange, and I just want to do a good job, be as thorough as possible. I get a bad feeling about some people; they almost make me worry, the way they walk by all the things in the store, not even seeing them, just keeping their distance. They only want to look at price tags and don't get any pleasure at all out of being surrounded by so many beautiful things. They go to a department, head straight for the saleslady, and ask for one specific item, as if they can't risk being seduced by some other beautiful thing. They buy cheap, tasteless stuff. They're also the ones clinging to their purses: they're more interested in their money than what their money can buy. And then there are the women I see week after week, in the same department in the same store, always staring at the same thing. Maybe it's something fairly expensive, so they're saving their money a little at a time. Or maybe they're working themselves up to buying something, making sure it's exactly right.

So far, I have to admit, this has all been fairly easy to talk about, to describe. I'll circle someone, trying to establish a sort of mental connection, but making as little real contact as possible. We can't look each other in the eye; if we do, it's over. Sometimes I test myself, almost draw up next to her; I examine what she's just examined; I try to move like she moves; I look where she's looked. This is very important—to read her, I need to identify with her. The more I feel I'm succeeding, the more I enjoy myself, and also, no matter how strange this might sound (the two of us, we live worlds apart), it's my way of getting to know someone. I can feel incredibly close to someone. Unfortunately, I'm pretty shy, and I can't maintain this feeling very long. It's so overpowering, there comes a time when it's almost unbearable: I can hardly control this desire to make some contact beyond what's necessary to earn my living. Sometimes, it happens. I'll chat with the person a little—you know how it is in a store—about what's in front of us, about matching colors or something, and then I'll take off. On these rare occasions, all I'm left with is the feeling that in just one moment, I've blown a half hour's work, that with a few banal, clichéd phrases, I've cheapened a real closeness, an affection I could have savored in an entirely different way. It's just beautiful watching someone (from the outside, if I can phrase it that way) who's drawn by her desire, who touches the fabrics, and smells the drop of perfume on her wrist, and tastes the moisturizing cream with the tip of her tongue. Department stores are easy places to work; they're fascinating, too, and here's why: they're like gardens of delight, and that's just beautiful. I know you understand. I've seen the way you move, the way you look.

All pleasure must come to an end. My pleasure, my dream life of watching another vibrant person, ends with a theft. It's quick, it's ugly, it's dark; it blots out everything else. I think this is typically male— breaking things off in such an ugly way. The theft itself is hard to describe: something, almost a different self, will take its revenge, and when this self retreats, so do its memories. Now I'm here in my rented room, and all that's left is a pure chain of events. Like the workings of a machine. I move toward the purse, take it, put it in a larger bag I always carry, and the whole time, I'm walking away. I move quickly, calmly; I try to act natural. After I've left the room or I'm blocked from view behind some shelves, I hurry to the exit. I don't look back— I don't want to be noticed—but I keep my ears open. Outside, I run to the first corner, the first bar, the first subway stop. In cooler weather,

I'll keep a bright-colored jacket or sweater in my bag that I'll slip on to change my appearance. In an hour I'm home; then I'll take a look at what I've got. During that hour, my fear keeps building, but as soon as I step inside my door, it disappears, and all I feel is incredibly weak and tired.

The two letters I found in your purse also piqued my interest because they were typed but didn't seem like business letters or anything official. After I read them, I thought that maybe the person typed them because he was shy, or even a little deceitful. I liked the idea of someone who didn't want to show his handwriting. Let me clarify here that the letter you're reading now is only typed because it's practical. For years I was a secretary, so I'm more comfortable using a typewriter than a pen. I think we all get an immediate impression from someone's handwriting, like we get from someone's face or body or clothes. And I think we all have a certain amount of natural talent that can be developed, when put to use. I really got a feeling from these typed letters: as I said before, that they're typed means someone's hiding something; and then I was struck by that wide left margin, like a person who pauses between each little burst of speech; and the lines run to the end of the page—some run right off the page, mutilated, the way some people end their sentences by mumbling, garbling their words. I'm not trying to do some cheap graphology here; these analogies just help me explain my first impressions. I don't know if you can make direct correlations between the psychology behind certain speech patterns and their effect on the listener.

As I already explained, I read your letters mostly out of a sense of duty, but I also can't deny that I was curious. It did feel like I was violating a trust, though, and something more complicated, too, not just from a moral stand point, but because of the head games involved: because stealing a purse, what I do for a living, ultimately helps me, while I read your letters to see if they helped you; and a person's gratuitous interest in how useful something is for someone else makes that person, whether he knows it or not, something of a hypocrite. After reading your letters, I can't say exactly what I was hoping to find; probably something interesting, at least interesting enough to keep me reading. For a while, I remember thinking they were love letters. But this is silly: you know perfectly well who wrote these letters, and of course you understand them a lot better than I do. I don't think I could write a love letter—I've never tried, anyway—the situation's never come up. I've seen a lot of how-to books or collections of love letters on store shelves, and it's got me thinking, though maybe this isn't reasonable, that the people who write love letters can't actually handle any real emotion. And this must be extremely painful and sad.

One letter describes a garden, the other, a room. The descriptions are very precise, but your friend (I'm assuming he's your friend) seems to think everything's a mystery. I'm tempted to show you what I mean by quoting from some of the more interesting passages, the ones that made me decide to write you in the first place. But I'd rather not—it's embarrassing—and I think you'd find it pretty unpleasant, too. But I don't want to paraphrase, either: I'd feel like one of those pesky salespeople who keeps interrupting with stupid, phony comments like, Look how green! How yellow! How round! How light!, as if we're all completely deprived of our senses.

Maybe I should limit myself to how I reacted to your letters instead of discussing the letters themselves. But I've only just realized now that I can't separate the two at all. In short, these letters seem as if they're written by someone from an unfinished place, and only the people who live in this place can actually finish it, by letting their imaginations run wild. I don't know if your friend's joking or serious, if he's sick or sane (sorry to be blunt), if he's master or servant to this imaginary world he describes so well. He describes some photos tacked to the wall: *These photos, even the ones that are the most touching and evocative to the person who put them up, are actually a little silly and pretentious. They suffer a great deal because they're old, and they mock each other for it; the oldest have to endure the sneers of those just tacked up the other day. Slowly, the oldest photos are slipping away, into the past, withering, their corners curling; desperate, they try to commit suicide, tearing themselves off the wall, plummeting headlong to the floor, trying to whisk beneath the couch, to disappear from this life, from all the others and their insults. Meanwhile, the youngest ones heckle and jeer at these foolish attempts to escape, and the other old photos grow quiet, hoping not to be the next victims . . .*

In another passage, he describes a friend just waking up: *Stefano in bed, barely awake, no, not awake yet, in that half-stage between sleeping and waking, when his soul hasn't taken over his body again, and his body's still just a soft, white mound of flesh. Sleep fills his entire body, every cell, and though his body can move, can walk around in the room, this isn't a man walking; this is a gathering of clouds, and all it would take is just one breath to scatter the clouds away. Then the soul drops from the sky, crashes through the ceiling, a whirlwind that tears the room apart, a wind blowing into Stefano's heart, swelling his heart, pushing out sleep, rolling in his blood, flowering in his mind, opening his mind to another day, you can see it in his eyes now, his soul, still smelling of sky and stars, a memory of the divine, mingling with the scent of Stefano's warming flesh.*

Your friend has an odd way of seeing things that don't exist, that are absent, and seeing them just as intensely, perhaps more intensely, than things that do exist, that are actually there; he seems full of emotion, full of passion, love, and also fear, feelings completely out of proportion to the things and real events that probably provoked them in the first place. I truly believe that for every situation, every person experiences different sensations, sensations that vary in content, quality, and strength; but that doesn't mean we all live in entirely separate worlds. Anyway, though your friend's descriptions were completely unreal, I took to them at once. Children view reality this way, too, and I'm not sure if it's instinct or habit that makes adults tell fairytales and stories to reinforce this idea of the world as somehow magical, or if adults are just too lazy to explain the way things really work. When I was four or five, my family lived in a town along the coast, and the sun, the summer heat, were absolutely awful. Our apartment had a very large terrace I used to play on, but it was too hot to go out there in the summer. On washdays, the laundry was always hung out to dry on this terrace. Then I'd go out; I was enchanted by all those white sheets, by the fresh laundry smell. The clotheslines ran parallel, taut between the walls, and in among the sheets, I was shut up in a small room that was cool and very bright. And I'd stay there, my senses taut, for quite some time. Who knows what was going through my mind. Something very emotional, I'm sure, some deep contemplation. Your friend talks about his Sunday mornings, how, since he doesn't have to work, he'll *go out to the garden after showering, have a cigarette and look at the plants, the leaves on the ground, the wall, the gravel. Once in a while,* your friend writes, *I think you're in the garden, too, and this thought is so intense that your soul, wherever you are, feels drawn here, and it leaves your body for just an instant, comes here looking for the person looking for it, sees me, waves, then slips back to you before you've even noticed it's gone, or maybe you have noticed, but your soul can't leave you all alone, so it's come home. This happens in an instant: but your soul, this quick come-stop-go, leaves something behind in the air, a waft of some imagined smell that mingles with the smells of the garden and gives off a feeling of joy that's also very good for the plants.* This could have just been some fantasy meant to charm you, but then your friend followed up with some serious, serious questions: what was it like not having your soul for a few seconds and did your soul by any chance tell you what happened on these quick trips.

The description about the red carpet stuck with me, too, because it did such a good job of making something feel real that really isn't: *To get from one side of the carpet to the other, you have to cross the entire world. You measure the carpet along the outside edge: 2.5 meters long. You climb on, start walking, you walk and you walk, and you see strange, wonderful places, forests, palaces, crowds, deserts, people of every race, animals of every kind, and every climate you can imagine: nothing can harm you, because you're on the carpet. In eighty days, you'll reach the other side. If you return, the carpet's so large you won't remember the right path, so one way or another, no trip's the same. But be careful getting off the carpet—if you don't pay attention, it's like jumping off a moving train—you'll crash against the wall of the room or find yourself in a different room entirely, someplace strange and hostile—*that's exactly how I felt when I suddenly stopped reading and found myself back in my rented room, which had always seemed so modest and comfortable before.

It sounds like I was warning you a little just then. I promise I don't want to get between you and your friend, though in a way, I guess I am butting into your conversation. I figured since you kept these letters in your purse, you must enjoy having them with you, close at hand, these descriptions of another world almost (or perhaps I should say *memories* of another world, almost). And then I started thinking that in spite of how you look—or from what I could tell, anyway, because you seemed so happily grounded—that maybe you really belong to another world, too. I've asked myself if just being physically exposed to these letters could really change the way I see things. I've thought about it and I've thought about it, and I have to confess, I've toyed with trying to shame myself out of thinking this way. I almost feel as though your letters have taken me hostage, drawn me in with their incongruous, unreal, twisted logic, and this abduction, this small, fantastic break-in, while entertaining, has also left me with an awareness of danger hanging over me.

I'm a person with his feet on the ground, and I try only to allow myself thoughts and feelings that let me live how I want to live. These letters you carried around like amulets were just too alien. Destroying them wouldn't free me, either. It feels right returning them: they're yours. But unfortunately, by telling you what's in my heart, I don't believe I've explained myself at all. I'm writing this letter because it takes a letter to be free of a letter, the way it takes a love to be free of a love, or a dream to be free of a dream. But what does it take to free yourself from someone else's dreams?

I'll let you in on a little secret. I once loved a girl very much. Maybe it was passion more than love—there wasn't much thought involved. We couldn't see each other a whole lot. I'd visit her on Sundays, and we'd be together a couple of hours. We didn't really talk: we didn't know how to talk to one another. We weren't all that happy, but we were as happy as we allowed ourselves to be. One day, all of a sudden, she called me a totem: "That's what you are—a totem."

And at that moment, I think I felt like I'd been transformed into some imaginary being, something protective and menacing at the same time. I tried to make a joke of it, stuck my fingers up behind my head like feathers. But that was a mistake. It was the beginning of the end, a quick and painful ending to our weak love. I don't know if all this is good or bad. I do know—I've learned—that in my particular case, there's only one possible world, and that's the world you see with your eyes open; the other world, the one you see with your eyes closed, is too dangerous a place. I just wrote "we" and "our" as if I knew now or had any idea then of what was going on in this girl's mind, or in her heart. Of course that's not possible.

As you probably imagined, I didn't write this long letter all in one sitting. I've corrected things, revised things, added things. In some parts, the tone seems different, even ugly; other parts are just digressions that can't possibly interest you. The letter's too long, I know this, and if I kept it a few more days, it would be longer still. I'm taking advantage of your time, just as a few days ago, I unfortunately took advantage of your personal property. I suppose you're fairly annoyed with me. But you have to admit, at least I've tried not to make things any worse. And in spite of how long this letter is or all my efforts in writing it, I get a familiar feeling here. The most important thing I wanted to say, what I first announced, and hinted at, and promised over the course of a number of wandering pages (but you can't be concise when you have something important to say), in the end I've said very quickly, carelessly, almost in secret.

A great writer, in a letter he wrote to the woman he loved at the time, said a letter is "some kind of trail marker leading to a human creature, along a path where you grow happier with every step, until one bright moment when you realize you're not moving forward at all, just going round and round in your own labyrinth, only you're more excited, more confused than normal." I didn't quote this to make myself look smart; I think it's fitting. You might say that in some letters, maybe all letters, the important thing is only said after the final sentence, in the silence that follows. I'm very shy and reserved, and that's why I chose my line of work. There have been many times, during intense conversations full of affection and emotion, with people I loved very much or at least wanted to love very much, that my words slowly disappeared, until all I had left in my head was one tiny phrase, or a few phrases, incongruous, but full of meaning, mysterious phrases, impossible to say. And in those moments, you can almost hear your brain creaking, straining to raise too great a weight. To say these words, to transform their mystery into a simple sequence, compressions and decompressions of air, to hear them disperse, scattered, useless, this would have been too much.

As I stop writing this letter, I apologize to you that I can't even sign it. Good luck.

# *The Apprentice*

It's late June, not even eight in the morning, and already hot. The apprentice has already been to the newsstand and waits in front of the closed shop door holding a newspaper by one corner, between two fingers. He'd never think of leafing through the paper, or rolling it up, or using it to fan himself, to cool down or just pass the time, and he'd certainly never tuck it under his arm. He holds the paper by one corner, between two fingers, because every morning it's his job to get the new paper, and he wants the paper to maintain that quality of something new, something just made, like a rose just beginning to open, the petals still intact, the color still intense. The newspaper, warm from the sun, gives off a pleasant smell of paper and ink. When he hears a noise from inside (his boss lives above the workshop and is coming down the stairs), the apprentice jumps, and when he sees the door opening (two metal shutters held in place by a bar that the boss has just removed), he pulls wide the shutters with two precise movements of his left hand (the paper is in his right). He goes inside (come winter, they'll hang a wooden door here with a tiny window), and he gropes around (his eyes haven't adjusted yet) and gently lays the paper on the counter, then hurries to open the windows and let in the light. He finds yesterday's paper under the counter, tears out a few pages, and cleans the windows with alcohol, inside and out. Then he adjusts the Venetian blinds to block out any direct sun while bringing in the maximum amount of light (as the sun shifts, he'll go around and adjust the blinds a few more times; this is something the apprentice thought up on his own, those first sunny days, and no one had to ask: the workshop doesn't heat up as much; all told, readjusting the blinds takes maybe two minutes a day, and if the benefit is small, so is the effort involved: it all evens out).

In the bathroom, he fills the water bottle and sprinkles the sidewalk, then he sweeps, holding the millet broom at a sharp angle, to keep down the dust. Meanwhile, the boss has gone to the basement to turn on the main switches to the machines. The apprentice steps into the warehouse, an enormous space even larger than the shop; he takes the keys to the *motocarro* off the nail (as the boss starts up the machines, the shop is beginning to hum), and he goes out to the back courtyard, opens the gate, gets the small motorcycle-truck from the shed where he left it the night before, and he wheels it onto street, then parks it in front of the shop.

He heads back to the warehouse, to the large table running along an entire wall that holds parts ready for delivery. These parts are grouped together, an envelope with an invoice taped to one item per group. The invoice includes the customer's address, a description of the merchandise, the price, order number, payment method. Heavy wrapping paper and unfolded boxes are stored on plywood shelves under the table. A large can holds recycled Styrofoam packing peanuts. The apprentice carefully packs up the parts, making sure they correspond to the amount on the invoice and that he's not mixing up any orders. He divides the orders, large and small, according to various areas in town, then loads the *motocarro* for his first run. Meanwhile the workers have arrived in the shop, and now, along with the humming machines, comes the sound of tools, and the boss's voice assigning jobs, and machinery scraping the blocks of raw material. The apprentice catches the boss's eye and says: I'm going.

He speeds off, even if the *motocarro* is overloaded and skids a bit on the curves, but he watches out for potholes and manhole covers. He knows the town by heart; the clients are always the same, tiny businesses, usually on the edge of town. If the gate's closed, he rings a small bell, but it's almost always open; then he goes right in, and he knows exactly where to go, the warehouse or the shop, and he gets the invoice signed as a record of delivery; sometimes he has to wait five minutes for some scrupulous warehouse supervisor who wants to open the package and inspect the contents; then he runs to the office and gives the management a copy of the invoice. By now, they know him and greet him every place he goes, but he never stops and chats (unlike the other delivery boys); he always makes sure he's polite, says hello and goodbye and gives them a big smile, even on days he's tired or cranky, but he doesn't like wasting time, and hurries off.

At one place, there's an office girl who must be a little older than the apprentice; she has a page-boy haircut and very dark eyes, and she's very delicate. The apprentice thinks she's nice. Once in a while, he wishes he could get to know her, talk with her a little; but he's not sure how to go about it, with this girl he sees maybe once or twice a week, for a couple of minutes at a time; besides, a delivery boy's a delivery boy, and doesn't count for much; while he wouldn't think of falling behind by stopping and talking with this girl (and, really, she's the one who always starts it, commenting on this or that, trying to keep him there; he thinks she might like him, but he doesn't know why), when the apprentice sees her, he always has a few things to say (good morning, I left the order in the shop, they've already looked it over, here's the invoice, anything else? thank you, goodbye, have a nice day), and he tries not to sound too banal, tries to add a certain intensity so she can tell he likes her, but not when he's referring to work, not with words like merchandise, shop, invoice; no, he saves this for words tied directly or indirectly to her, the way he says hello, and puts the emphasis on *you* and the feminine endings of the words he uses with her. Sometimes, when the girl addresses him with the informal *tu*, he slips and calls her *tu* as well and immediately feels ashamed, but if a *tu* pops out, he won't correct himself: he doesn't want to make things any worse. The apprentice likes to use the formal *lei* at work, even, as often happens, with people his own age or just a little older: it's better that way, not to mention, he wants to save *tu* for friends outside work, for those relationships he has just for their own sake. Actually, sometimes he even uses the plural *voi*, to make it clear he's not exactly talking to the person standing in front of him, some- one he may never have met before, but that he's talking, abstractly, to the firm as a whole; he does this especially when he has something unpleasant to say, if someone's complaining that a delivery's a day late, for instance, and he has to explain that you—*voi*—can't call in an order at six o'clock the night before and expect it all there by nine the next morning; and they know this perfectly well, but for some reason, the apprentice thinks, they just have to make a scene every time, as if delays were the fault of lazy suppliers and not the occasional lack of foresight on the part of the acquisitions office. The apprentice uses *voi* with those people he finds unpleasant so he won't think of them as individuals, as people he doesn't like; this way, he can think of them as parts of the company, and he can stay indifferent, can even feel a little affection for them, because the apprentice knows that the cus- tomer must always be treated well, that the customer is what keeps the business running, and so the apprentice is extremely grateful.

The girl with the dark hair and dark eyes—she's a problem for the apprentice. She's a part of his job, so he has to treat her a certain way, but at the same time, he finds her attractive for reasons that have nothing to do with his job, and it feels awkward when she uses *tu* and tries to talk with him a little: he's on secure enough ground as long as their relationship is clear, a delivery boy and a secretary, but he feels a little lost when she speaks to him as though their relationship's not so clear after all, and then the apprentice gets lost in thinking about what might happen between them; and he also feels uncomfortable standing in front of this girl and being mistaken for a delivery boy instead of what he really is, what for him is much more interesting: an apprentice; he'd like it if she thought of him as an apprentice, but then he gets confused by this, because an apprentice doesn't quite exist in the present: he's more of a future person, so in the present, an apprentice is absent, and so right when the apprentice would like to have an enormous presence, he feels as though he's almost not there at all, and he'd rather cling to something safe, something certain, his position, though an error, of errand boy. And so he makes his delivery, says hello, and runs away.

After his first trip, the apprentice heads back to the shop, drops the signed invoices into the basket on the large warehouse table, and loads up the various packages for his next run: there aren't as many, just for a few clients downtown. He hurries to take the workers' orders; this is another of his assignments from the boss, getting cigarettes, a sandwich for anyone not going home. By now the apprentice knows the brand each worker smokes and what goes on his sandwich; but the apprentice still writes it all down on a scrap of paper, just in case. Then he climbs to the top of the inside stairs, knocks, and the boss's wife opens the door and tells him what stores he needs to go to; the boss's wife does her grocery shopping by phone, or if she visits a store herself, she always says: the boy will be by later. The apprentice rushes off, makes his few deliveries downtown, goes to the market square for cigarettes and sandwiches (the workers will pay him on their break), then picks up the things for the boss's wife. By the time he returns, he's out of breath: it's really hot now, and with the morning coming to a close, he can hardly believe how much work is left to do. First he climbs the stairs and brings the boss's wife her groceries, then he leaves the bag of cigarettes and sandwiches on the warehouse table. He knocks at the warehouse office and gets the outgoing mail from the boss: bills to send, registered letters with checks to their suppliers, bills to pay. The boss gives him the necessary funds, and the apprentice counts the money in front of him, and counts it again. In the warehouse, the orders from the day before are ready to mail, the packages addressed and stamped. The apprentice loads up everything and leaves. Sometimes he has to pick up boxes at the train station nearly across town. When he gets back, the workers are already eating and smoking in the warehouse, where it's cooler than the shop. They pay him for their sandwiches and cigarettes (he always makes sure he has the exact change ready), and he eats, too, but by himself, in the shade of the courtyard.

Mornings are pleasant. It's nice making his rounds, not a strain at all, even if he is always loading things and unloading things and climbing stairs and rushing around. The apprentice likes the idea of working fast: with an easy job like making deliveries, good means fast; he always makes sure he takes the fastest route; when he packs up orders, he's like a little robot, click, click, always the same, precise movements; though, really, he doesn't move like a robot: he's always thinking about every move he makes, even when it's repetitive, and he tries to perfect this movement, make it even faster, even more precise, in its own way, even more beautiful. Though he'd never tell anyone, the apprentice is sick to death of the clients thinking he's just a delivery boy; he's sick of the workers shouting to the foreman across the machine shop: here he is, here's Company _____'s delivery boy. He'd like to shout: not *delivery boy*—apprentice! I make deliveries because deliveries have to be made and someone has to do it and you can't expect the workers or the boss to do it, but I'm an apprentice, someone here to learn a job, so in a way, much more than a delivery boy, almost the promise of a worker, maybe even a skilled worker, or in time, the foreman of some large company, or maybe even the boss himself, running his own little business. A delivery boy's a delivery boy—a promise of nothing. Something else the apprentice doesn't like: doing errands for the boss's wife. He doesn't mind getting cigarettes and sandwiches for the workers: this seems like a politeness between co-workers, in its own small way, an opportunity to *be* co-workers, but the boss's wife, he can't stand her, also because she just assumes that if she needs something, he has to drop whatever work he's doing and run her errand; as if she didn't know, a boss's wife, that work is work, a serious thing; for a man, and even more for an apprentice, work comes first, above all else, even if it's unpleasant work, thankless work. The apprentice thinks even the boss doesn't like the way she takes advantage of his time; early on, even, when the boss told him he'd have to do her errands (which he said wouldn't be much, anyway), he also told the apprentice that they mustn't interfere with work, which is contradicted at every turn, especially during periods when there's so much work, so much, he's wiped out at night, back aching, feet boiling hot, and he doesn't want anything, not even food; during the winter, weeks have gone by when the apprentice hasn't seen any of his friends, he's just disappeared, spent Sundays wandering around the house, not going out, so tired he can't think—because he never does anything by rote, he's always thinking, always concentrating; when faced with some repetitive job that others would gladly do while gabbing away at the top of their lungs, he thinks about the job itself, stays very focused, so by the end of the day his mind feels empty, even though some ideas are stuck in his head, keep going round and round, won't let go, possess him, and then the only thing

to do is go to bed, there, there, try and sleep now, and try not to have
bad dreams.

When the workers are done eating, they go for an espresso at the
corner coffee bar, and the apprentice sweeps up the crumbs and cigarette butts: the warehouse has to be clean before work starts up again;
the apprentice won't have a coffee himself, even though he'd like one:
he could wash his homemade sandwich down with some coffee, keep
himself from growing sleepy in the ever-lurking heat; but he's figured
out the total for a coffee every day at work, and it adds up to more
than a third of one month's salary, so, over the course of a year, he
would spend ten whole days just working for coffee. That morning,
while the apprentice was out, the table was piled once again with parts
ready to pack up: on one side, those to be delivered in town tomorrow,
on the other, those going out by mail the same day. The larger ship-
ments going out by parcel post are in shopping carts that the workers
loaded piece by piece in the shop, then pushed into the warehouse.
The apprentice starts packing up more merchandise, first the parcel-
post orders, then those going out by regular mail, and other carts
come rolling in, still more packages for parcel post. He slides the following day's deliveries under the large table; parcel-post orders go on
the wooden bench. The apprentice works quickly, wraps up the parts
well, seals the boxes with brown packing tape, then ties them with
plastic banding, weighs them, glues on the address cards, fills out the
mailing forms, stamps them. Sometimes the boss sends him to buy a
few things or make a delivery if a client absolutely needs an order by
the end of the day. Other times, it's the boss's wife who wants him for
something, and the more obnoxious the errand, the faster, the harder
he works, because he really doesn't want to argue, and so he thinks
of it all as work and jumps right in: ready, set, go. His afternoon jobs
he doesn't care for; weeks earlier, the boss told the apprentice: when

you're done here, come and see me and I'll start your training; but he has so many packages, and sometimes the orders pile up, and there are days (though rarely) when the apprentice can't even finish the packages he has, and so, bit by bit, he keeps on working, and realizes he can't succeed, and he starts to feel desperate, despondent, and then just tries to shut his eyes and ears and think about what he's doing, and nothing more. Other times, though, when the apprentice does manage to finish, he goes and sees the boss, but the boss is always busy and snaps: not now.

Sometimes the boss will send him to one of the older workers. But this worker has his own job to do and just says: watch. While the apprentice pays careful attention, the workers are such experts, they move so fast, he can hardly tell what they're doing and can't understand what it all means. There are all kinds of small buttons and levers to push, and they all seem the same, and the worker doesn't even look while he pushes them; he just watches the monitor above the machine that shows the work going on inside. The apprentice doesn't dare ask any questions; he waits for the worker to stop a moment, to step back from the machine, but this never seems to happen. Once in a while, if the apprentice does try to ask something, the answer's always fairly rude: don't bug me, or: can't you see—what are you, blind? But while they work, the men are always talking among themselves: about soccer, and women, and politics, always joking, always kidding around, but never taking their eyes off the screen, not looking at each other, talking in droning voices, almost always (the apprentice noticed this after only a few days) talking about the same things; even a stupid joke can last for days; slowly, their talk fills the air, like cigarette smoke (nearly all the workers smoke); the walls repeat their words; they stagnate; there comes a time by afternoon when the workers barely speak; then all you hear in the shop are stagnant words, words already spoken, distracted words unheard by distracted ears, and so they linger in the enormous room. The apprentice keeps his eyes fixed on the workers' hands, but his ears that long to hear some sort of lesson are nearly overflowing with these stagnant words; and so, after a time, the apprentice jolts to as a worker turns and says in a different tone: you see? see how it's done? And the apprentice grows red with shame, astonished he's caught these scattered words, and he silently shakes his head no, and looks down, and feels like nothing. The apprentice doesn't know how to keep the workers' talk from filling his head, even though, when he thinks about it later, all this talk seems like blather, talking just to hear yourself talk, and often dirty besides; but it's how men talk, or at least how he thinks men talk, and the apprentice really wants to be a man, a grown man, a worker, able to do everything he sees the workers doing, and that means cracking dirty jokes, getting worked up over soccer, talking about how bad it is in Italy, it's so hard to take, it's just exhausting, and saying this over and over, always blaming somebody, this all-powerful, mysterious somebody that no one understands, though he's right there, under our noses. He's disgusted by the workers' talk, but drawn to it as well; it fills his ears; he can't seem to tear himself away; he listens closely, as he'd listen to some rich, precise, on-the-job training. And so, though he's barely had any time to watch and listen, when the boss pops in and tells the workers it's time to finish up, turn off the machines, and get ready to close, the apprentice, who rushed around all afternoon just to stay in the shop a little longer and watch and learn, now feels as though a great weight has been lifted, he feels happy, and while the workers stretch, collect their things, and say goodbye to one another, the apprentice races to the basement, grabs the bucket of sawdust, and quickly, carefully, sweeps the floor: he's figured out the exact right strokes for every corner of the large room, he knows where the dirt accumulates, and in a few minutes he's done, then he wheels the *motocarro* back to the courtyard shed, hangs the keys on the nail, shouts: goodbye!, and goes.

This is what the apprentice thinks at the start of his summer break. It's his first vacation as a worker, so his first *real* summer break. But how can he possibly be on summer break—it's such a waste of time—all of a sudden, on vacation, even if he's unprepared, doesn't want one; life in the shop is so absurd: month after month of frenetic work, then— click—close it all up. Never time to teach him anything, but let's close up for a month. It would be great having a month of half-time, maybe just opening the shop for half the day, but no chasing after clients (everything's closed in August, anyway: let them wait); he could focus on all those things he never gets to during the year. There's a ton of work: the building is ancient, and there are two connected store- rooms, one older than the other, that need to be organized, cleaned out, renovated; then there are so many small things, too, like sprucing up the men's bathroom, making it halfway decent; plus, a month off, without production always buzzing in their ears, would mean time for training, and training is everything to an apprentice; it's his nature, so to speak, his reason for being; and since you can't produce at full tilt and train someone, too, here's the perfect time, the ideal time, summer time. But no: everything's closed up, and once in a while, the apprentice will bike through town, past the shop, almost hoping he'll find it open, that he'll see someone inside, but of course it's closed; the boss and his wife are off somewhere on vacation, and the building is empty as empty can be: silent, sleeping. It's strange watching the building, like spying on someone sleeping, his breathing, his uncon- scious movements, and this feels rude, but also oddly stirring, exciting even, and so, in a way, the apprentice thinks, slightly abnormal and perverse. The apprentice is ashamed by his secret visits to the shop, and whenever he goes by, he always thinks up some excuse in case he runs into anyone, something that will justify his being there, though of course he's made the trip on purpose, to see the shop, to make sure it's still there, that he hasn't been forgotten.

So summer ends; winter has come.

One morning, a worker doesn't show up. He calls in sick, has a fever and a cough. A little later his wife drops by with a doctor's note: at least five days' bed rest, another five days at home. After the break, when the apprentice is back in the warehouse, packing up orders like usual, the boss comes over and says: get on that machine. The apprentice, who worried all morning about exactly this, answers: but I don't know how to run it. The boss: you've seen it done plenty—now move. Then, over his shoulder, heading back to the office: at least he's better than nothing. Which makes the apprentice furious: he's certainly much more than nothing, even if he doesn't know what. Scared stiff, he approaches the still-cold machine that's been off all morning; he turns it on, pushes the buttons in the order he's seen them pushed so many times; with every button, he hesitates, which of course makes absolutely no sense: because every time you turn on the machine, this is how you push the buttons, there's no other way: so how could he possibly be doing it wrong? And even if he is doing it wrong, pushing the wrong button lightly won't make it any less wrong, or any less pushed.

The order is taped beneath the monitor: some of one piece, some of another; the apprentice has seen both pieces made many times. All around him, the workers are strangely quiet at their machines; there's none of the usual chatter in the room, as if they suddenly felt the presence of this stranger, this liar, this pretender claiming to be a worker instead of what he really is: a simple apprentice, someone still learning, and learning is very different from doing, just a little game for a little apprentice-boy; doing is something for men, and he's no man. The apprentice can hear the hostility in all this silence, can see it in all their faces: look, see what's in store for us—we'll get sick with something, nothing, and we'll have to stay home a few days, and when we come back, here's some kid on our machine, doing a lousy job, but he's cheaper for the boss, and suddenly, we'll grow old, and start to die. The apprentice, confused, all in a muddle, tries to defend himself: I'm not the one who chose to start like this, he thinks; I wanted to learn a little at a time, to learn from you: I respect you all so much; I'm not the one who chose to step in all of a sudden; the truth is, I'm afraid I'll look bad, get sent back to packing boxes—maybe not even that—maybe the boss will realize I still haven't learned a thing, and he'll send me away entirely, get some other apprentice; I'm not the one who chose this—I didn't have a choice—if the boss says do something, I do it—who am I to argue with the boss? On the other hand, I am an apprentice, here to learn, and sooner or later, I'll take the place of one of you: feel free, *signori*, to keep from growing old, to keep your arms, your eyesight strong; go ahead, if you want and if you can; I have to follow my own path, and there's nothing wrong with that, especially since I'm only following orders; you yourselves took someone's place as well.

This is what he's thinking while the machine warms up, and he gets a block of raw material from the cart and puts it in the chute, as he's seen it done so many times; he lays the block down gently, as he'd lay a newborn baby in a crib, supporting the head, holding, not squeezing. Then he presses the button that makes the block slide down the chute, as he's seen it done so many times, and when he hears the noise of the block against the utensil inside the machine (at least that's what he thinks this noise means), he starts pushing the buttons in the order he's seen the worker push them on that machine so many times; he hears the noise of the utensil attacking the block, a noise with no reprieve—what's cut is cut—for a moment, it's hard to tell how long, there's only this noise; then he realizes he's watching the control panel, not the screen; he's working blind. You should never watch just the control panel! He jerks his head up to the monitor: the utensil has sliced a useless rectangle from the block, and not a small one, either. He studies the control panel, releases the utensil, the noise stops. With the utensil freed, he works the buttons again and again, not looking at the control panel. He knows the measurements of the finished pieces, and the monitor screen shows where the utensil is, its every move. The apprentice keeps his eye on the center of the screen, but this is wrong: he should be watching the lower part of the screen, the columns of changing numbers; the image at the center, a schematic of the utensil against the block of raw material, isn't detailed enough for such precise work. The apprentice starts over, guides the utensil step by step, raising it from the block after every move; and so he makes a nearly perfect piece, with just this one edge that (luckily) sticks out, so maybe he can shave it off by running the piece through the machine a second time.

The apprentice cuts another piece, and this one's really pretty good. He checks the time: an hour's passed, and he knows perfectly well that a worker makes a piece nearly every five minutes: he's cut one good piece, one flawed piece, and he's wasted some raw material—in an *hour*! He'll never be able to do the job, he tells himself, just by copying someone else's moves; there must be some sort of intrinsic logic here that no one ever explained; every movement must be made in some precise way, for some precise reason that no one ever told him; the entire art of it lies hidden; there's only mechanized movement, man and machine. While the apprentice is thinking this, he sends another block through and, barely paying attention, produces another piece, this time perfect, and he checks the clock: only ten minutes. At least I'll show him, thinks the apprentice, that I'm not such a nothing after all, and right then, while he's moving the block forward a little more, he sees the boss's wife come down the stairs, go into the warehouse, and start packing boxes.

His job! They can't take that away, he thinks, when he doesn't even have this one yet; then all at once, he's almost glad that the boss's wife, that woman who wasted his time with all her stupid errands and didn't even look at him when she ordered him around, that now she's the one stuck doing his job, the job of the new guy, who can't do anything; she's not going on the machine—not her! Meanwhile he's finished two more pieces and has to load up another block; he tries a fast maneuver and hurts himself, gets his right index finger caught under the block in the chute, and though it barely bleeds, it hurts—the finger tip's almost numb. The apprentice doesn't even say ouch, just tucks his index finger under his thumb, hits the buttons with his middle finger, and keeps on going. Then he notices that the other workers are chatting peacefully among themselves, like always, as if nothing's changed, and this feels almost like a truce, and suddenly he's happy, and he listens to them talking, and ruins a piece. Furious, he tries to block them out, to close his ears, glue his eyes to the screen, ignore his smashed, pulsing finger, just watch the numbers and push the keys, keep it up. By the end of the day, he's made nineteen good pieces, and ruined four. The boss has come by twice and not said a word; that evening he says: tomorrow morning, make your deliveries like normal—my wife put them together—in the afternoon, you'll work here. The next day, the apprentice does twenty-six pieces right, and ruins two. He's all smiles, and the boss tells him: quit wasting so much material. The apprentice focuses as hard as he can, concentrating on his machine and nothing else, and he goes home exhausted, has no interest in eating, or seeing his friends, or going to the movies. After a week, he makes thirty-two pieces in an afternoon and doesn't waste any material, and he starts wondering what will happen when the sick worker comes back. The worker comes back, and the apprentice returns to his big boxes and his little boxes, and no one says a word, as if nothing's changed. He's behind, even, can't seem to catch up.

The apprentice has grown to love his boss. The boss owns his future, so the apprentice loves him. For the most part, the boss is in his office with his bookkeeping, his calculations, his sales reps. Sometimes you can hear him in there yelling at sales reps, or he's on the phone, yelling at clients and suppliers: over some payment that hasn't come, or because the orders are just trickling in, or the reps keep fawning over the same old clients and of course they're promising minimum prices and endlessly delayed payments and they're too lazy to drum up any new business. No one's particularly impressed at the boss's ranting, not the workers, not the reps who just put up with it, and certainly not the clients and the suppliers who are used to everything and pay when they feel like it and place their orders when they're good and ready and expect their deliveries right away. The boss is always yelling about the same things, especially that he can't take it anymore: when it comes down to it, he's got his little savings, and if things keep going like this, he's shutting the place down and retiring, and he'll just stick to gardening and watching sports on TV. No one pays any attention, especially those workers who've been in the shop forever and have heard this stuff over and over; the apprentice is the only one who worries, not because he thinks the business is in any real danger—he can tell the boss is singing the same old song—but because he knows the boss might just do it someday, just close up on a whim, and then the apprentice and the workers and the sales reps can all kiss their jobs goodbye. It might never happen, but it could happen: and this, the apprentice knows, is what it means to be dependent: my job, boss, is a huge part of my life, and it's in your hands, and your hands don't even care; they could just open at any time, for no good reason, just a whim, a distraction, and let my life slip away; and for this reason, boss, you're like some strange, rough, tiny god; but to me, a teeny-tiny apprentice, you're great and powerful; and I love you, because when it comes to gods, you either love them or you hate them, and I can't hate; I love you as much as an apprentice can love, this creature whose whole reason for being is to learn, to take in lessons and return them in thought and deed. One mistake from the boss, disaster strikes, but this just can't happen: the boss is the boss; he's not like other mortals who make mistakes from time to time; for the apprentice, it's simply impossible that the boss could make a mistake. But the workers, those idiots on their machines, they don't seem to realize the boss is divine—just the opposite—they swear at him behind his back, say the worst possible things—clearly, every one of them thinks he could run the shop just as well, or better; they're so pretentious, so arrogant, and they don't even know it; they're certainly not cut out to be bosses— they don't have the stomach for it, they're not hungry for it—just look at them, the apprentice thinks, and you can tell they stopped being apprentices long ago; they aren't capable of learning (if they ever were), all they can do is memorize a sequence of actions, repetitious behaviors; they don't even know how to talk; all they can say is: look. They don't possess any knowledge that can be said in words; all they have left is matter, motion.

The apprentice is glad to have his work. But there are mornings he'd rather not go in, when it takes all his effort just to get out of bed, when his back aches, especially his lower back, and he feels like he's late even if the clock says otherwise, and his muscles have gone numb, his hands don't work right, his eyes won't focus, his belly feels bloated. On those mornings, all his flesh seems to be begging him not to go in, to stay in bed, though he still feels bad in bed, but at least in bed there isn't work; in bed, he's like a sick child with a stack of old comic books and a worried mama. On these mornings, the apprentice knows if he doesn't snap to, if he doesn't hurry, he'll stay locked inside this uncertainty, this disgust that's there for no real reason. What's important is getting through the first few hours, and then the day goes by practically on its own; luckily, he pretty much does the same things every day and, luckily, he's almost always out and about in the morning; he sees things, people: so even on the worst days, even if it takes all his effort, the apprentice can still work.

And he's glad to have his work, even on those days he's filled with disgust: as if work itself were cause for happiness beyond feeling sick or well. The apprentice thinks: I have my work, a loving home, so why should I feel unhappy? And he tries to keep these two things separate in his mind, this disgust that seems to come entirely from within, almost like the product of some long-forgotten evil dreams that still live on, mysteriously, in his flesh, and this happiness he can't deny—he'd be a fool to try—because it reflects the physical reality of his life. To the apprentice, despising life is just about the stupidest thing you can do—what's the point?—better to take life as it comes, to figure out a way to block these feelings of disgust, or when you're overwhelmed by disgust, to recall something happy; to lose yourself to disgust, this, yes, this disgust can hold back happiness, can shift from work to people to things to places, can invade everything. But freeing yourself from disgust is fairly easy; the apprentice can easily free himself: working a few hours wakes up your flesh, expels what's left of evil dreams, and for this reason the apprentice is glad for work, especially during those hours of the morning when he can get some exercise; if he thinks about it, work is almost a cure, that's what he often thinks, but it's not the reason, not the whole reason the apprentice is glad for work. What really makes him happy is the effort it requires. Once in a while, the apprentice dreams of a time when he might not have to work anymore, when he can spend his days lost in laziness without evil dreams or burdens. But he knows, in the real world, that being lazy is another thing entirely from being happy: if the body's inactive, the flesh can't ward off feelings of disgust; in fact, it's generally on Sunday nights or holidays that the apprentice succumbs the most, when he can barely protect himself from these assaults. The apprentice knows that work is a punishment; he learned it at catechism when he was just a child: Adam and Eve were driven from earthly paradise for wanting to be like god, and they were condemned to toil for everything they needed, condemned, in other words, to work. In earthly paradise, the apprentice thinks, everything must have been within your grasp; idleness must have been beautiful, free from any threat of disgust. The apprentice is glad for this punishment of having to work; this seems like the proper remedy, the proper cure, like a sick person takes his medicine: why would he refuse? But the apprentice feels a little afraid when he notices that work is going well, when work pulls him away from his disgust: if he enjoys his work, it's not a punishment. The apprentice is convinced if people like to work, if they find it satisfying, then they've made a grave mistake; these people, he thinks, will work their entire lives without gaining the most important thing they can from work, what follows punishment: freedom from sin, and so, the happiness to come. The apprentice is convinced his happiness, which has grown fairly resilient from withstanding repeated attacks of disgust, is still hardly anything at all in comparison to the happiness he'll find when his punishment is through. Since punishment is good, the apprentice knows he has to accept it for what it is; trying to take the effort and exhaustion out of work would be like trying to take the saltiness out of salt. The apprentice can hardly stand how slow, how careless the workers are on those rare occasions when the boss is gone: he's very much aware, as he packs up orders in the warehouse, that they're bringing him less, that they're just throwing the stuff in the carts, that the voices coming from the workshop are louder, happier. They should be serving out their punishment with care, the apprentice thinks, with a solicitous love, not empty sentiment, with the love you feel when you're striving for a higher purpose, and finding happiness is most definitely a higher purpose; it's not petty, not selfish, not just a matter of one person's happiness: it concerns the happiness of humankind, from Adam and Eve onward.

One day the boss says: we need to take on another apprentice. And for a couple of weeks, boys keep coming in, usually the workers' nephews, or their cousins' sons, or their cousins' nephews, because the boss prefers some sort of family connection, but not too much of one; he says no to a worker who wants his son brought in (the apprentice also has a family connection: one of the workers is his father's cousin, a cousin he'd never actually met before he started in the shop, so his father had to describe him in minute detail so the apprentice wouldn't seem rude): some of the boys are small and timid, and they speak too softly, they have to be taken into the warehouse or out onto the street just to be heard; others are big and cocky; they're loud and they smoke; they stand outside the warehouse office, waiting for the boss to get off the phone, and they're already friendly with the workers, tossing off just the right comment, swearing like they were born to it. The apprentice is afraid of these big young guys: they've only just gotten there, they're nothing but pretenders, and they're already taking liberties he'd never dream of taking though he's been there almost a year; shut inside the office with the boss, they talk in raised voices, and the apprentice listens and thinks back to his first day: the boss took him into the office and gave him a long speech about work, about life, about a lot of things, and didn't ask him any questions (apparently, the family connection was all that mattered); and when the boss finally stopped talking and was quiet, the apprentice, the words catching in his throat from keeping quiet so long, told the boss: I'm here to learn, and I won't know how to do anything at first, but I'll do my best. At home they scolded him for not making a better impression, but two days later the boss called to say he'd take him on, that he was getting the paperwork together right away, because, the boss said, he seemed like a serious boy.

This small victory was somewhat troubling: it seemed impossible that it took so little effort, almost no effort, just presenting himself in all his weakness and availability; and it was also troubling, shocking, that his family and the workshop boss had such different opinions of him. By instinct, the boy put more stock in what his family thought: after all, his family really knew him, had produced him (so to speak) from top to bottom; he'd almost been tempted to show up at the workshop and tell the boss: look, you don't want me; I don't know how to do anything; on the other hand, this recognition that he had some value came from the outside (even if the boy couldn't really tell what that value was; he figured it would become clear in time, though: in a way, the boy entrusted the boss with this task; it was the boss who'd seen something in him, and it was the boss who'd show him his value, who'd guide him through his apprenticeship, toward maturity), and this was comforting, made him feel, for the first time, not so much that he was outside, but counter to his family, that he was capable of growing in unforeseen ways independent of his family; for the first time, he could think of himself as something other than a son: he was a real apprentice, a beautiful word, full of the future, the opposite of "son," a word made up entirely of the past.

The apprentice has the ability to take every event of his life as some kind of lesson for the future, especially when he can't seem to find even a trace of a lesson at the time; the dullness of something, the very lack of meaning, is almost a sign (an absent sign) of what it means; and so the apprentice throws himself into these meaningless events, hoping he'll find some small chasm, some mystery revealed, something new and thrilling. The apprentice knows you can only make sense of something after it's happened, and the only time you can glimpse any sort of meaning is when something's happened more than once, and even so, every time something happens it still carries a new lesson, if for no other reason than that the person doing the learning is always different, different in his mind, and his body, and his heart, just as water, since it's always water, is always different water dripping from the faucet. And because he's able to think this way, the apprentice treats every event in his life, even if it seems disagreeable, or degrading, or dangerous at the time, as one fragment of a lesson that will come together in the end and reveal itself as ordered, finished, justified: it's up to him, the apprentice, the one whose reason for being is to learn, to put the parts of this lesson together and not reject any of them from the start; and in this work, perhaps, the apprentice will find the path that seems to go on and on but that isn't difficult (a person is carried down this path, he can't be forced: day after day, event after event, and it doesn't take the slightest human effort; even when he sleeps, his dreams are full of instructive things, marvelous things), and this path will lead to maturity, to the point where he clearly understands this final order. And in this way, naturally, the apprentice finds maturity endlessly drawing away from him in time, and of course he has his doubts because, in spite of all his effort at loving all the events of his life, there are still those things he can only think of as disagreeable, degrading, or painful, and there are so many things that don't seem to have the slightest hint of a lesson, that don't prepare him at all to take things as they come, one thing after the other, and then at night, and more so on the days he isn't working, on Sunday mornings, for instance, they're all there, in his brain and in his gut, waiting for him, demanding a sense of order now, today, and not in some indefinite future.

Of the boys who show up in the workshop, the apprentice prefers the ones who are small and silent, not because he thinks they're like him (because he's fairly small and silent), but because they seem more pliable, easier to train to carry out a precise series of movements; in short, they seem like they'd make good, conscientious workers, and might even come to understand the meaning of dependence, something the other workers lack, that's lost on them. The apprentice can see himself teaching one of these boys the simple, but rigorous, indispensable things he's done for almost a year, and he likes the idea that through his words, he can train the body to act, to follow through on something, and he can train the mind to act, to obey swiftly, without effort. In the end, the boss chooses a big loud boy, and when this boy comes in, the boss tells the apprentice: show him what you do. Suddenly, even though he's so prepared, the apprentice feels strange, feels so small and awkward with all these things he's studied and learned so carefully, and yet he's supposed to train this boy who walks around this new place like he was born here; still, the apprentice throws himself into his explanations; he takes the boy around the workshop and the warehouse; he shows him everything, how he organizes his day, how to pack up orders to perfection; he shows him the wall map of the town, the fastest routes to all their major customers: in front of this bold, beefy boy, what he knows seems trivial, futile, but he tries his hardest to transform his knowledge into words that might sink into memory, so then, at just the right moment, these words can be drawn out again, to trigger actions, precise movements; he tries his hardest, and is outraged by this boy who's clearly not paying any attention, who's superficial and utterly lacking in imagination.

At a certain point, the apprentice pops his head into the boss's office and asks: what now? should I make the deliveries? The boss says: yeah, you go; have the other boy come here. The apprentice leaves, but he's later than normal and has to rush on his first trip, and when he returns, he sees that the new boy is in the workshop, and a worker is showing him how to run the machines, how to load a block onto the chute, how to work the utensil while keeping an eye on the monitor. The apprentice has to run even faster, he's late, and the morning's nearly through; when he starts taking sandwich orders, the new boy doesn't even look up, just shouts to him: cheese on mine, and a pack of _____, like he already knew someone came by every day to get all the orders for sandwiches and cigarettes.

After a week, the apprentice realizes that the boss wants him to keep doing what he's always been doing, from the very first day, while the new boy is clearly destined for real work; he'll go on the machines: he's already putting in eight hours a day, and no one's too busy to train him; they all have the time; even the boss devotes himself to the boy's training with a patience that makes the apprentice desperately jealous: he wants this, too, realizes he's never gotten the same treatment. This new boy, he'll become a worker—he practically was one the moment he showed up for his interview—meanwhile, the apprentice might be stuck in this half-life indefinitely. But he also understands that he doesn't have the slightest interest in becoming a worker: the short time he replaced the man out sick, he realized how repetitive this work was, how stupid and exhausting; he remembers coming home at night and not feeling like doing anything, barely wanting to eat, his back so stiff (from tension more than effort) that even lying in bed was painful; he's impressed by how quickly the new boy has become one of them, indistinguishable from the other workers, and this gets him thinking that there must be something about the worker's trade, something mysterious, invisible, that reduces brain capacity and locks a person inside a few predictable movements, a few thinkable thoughts; the apprentice is very much aware that there won't be an apprenticeship for this boy, there won't be a time when he's pushed with exercises, tasks, and orders, to see what emerges, what he can do; while I, the apprentice thinks, won't have a time after apprenticeship, a time to fulfill my potential. I'm in an apprenticeship without a future, a school without exams or diplomas, an endless contemplation without mastering a thing. They haven't turned me into an eternal child or an inexperienced adult, but something in between, something extremely productive: I'm a permanent apprentice, and a permanent apprentice has no definite form, is inexhaustible, can take on any form required and make this temporary form seem real, as if it's always been his coherent state. The apprentice feels himself being carried far away, sunk in chaotic, unbearable thoughts. He finds it extremely difficult to work: everything he does seems an end in itself, limited, stripped of meaning, of any logic he could live by; he doesn't do one thing that helps him in his life—everything seems like a subtraction of time and effort (physical, mental) from his life; suddenly he feels he needs to defend his life, even if he doesn't quite know what that life is, and sometimes while he works, he almost staggers with confusion: his head is filled with thoughts that follow from his work, that drive him back, that pull away from everything, thoughts that explore, with deep uncertainty, the meaning and nature of his life—of every life—of the movement he's just made with his right hand.

# On the Publication of My First Book

Ladies and Gentlemen,

I can't tell you how pleased I am to be here. Hello, everyone. I wanted to greet a number of you in person, but I see now that some of you slipped by in all the confusion. My apologies. As you might imagine, I'm pretty confused myself. I'm feeling embarrassed and pleased at the same time, embarrassed, perhaps, because I'm not able to take in so much pleasure all at once. Thank you.

Now I should say something about my book—my first book, that is, since it's pretty clear, as everyone keeps telling me, that I'll practically have to write another, and then another, and another. Just the idea of it sounds scary, and I get embarrassed when someone wants to know what I'm working on right now. A lot of people treat me like I think writing is the most important thing I do, as if it's my duty, practically my reason for being. I have to admit I've brought this up because I'd really rather not talk about it, and because there have been some very important things for me, in these past months, that had nothing to do with writing, and I don't really consider myself a professional writer, or that I'll become one in the future. I explained all this to somebody once when he asked me the fairly typical question, what I think comes first, life or art. I'm not even sure what that question means exactly—all I know is I feel constrained to stay in my life, that this is a chore that fills my days. If I'm embarrassed by certain situations or questions, maybe that's because I'm really not sure how to think of what I've done as "art"—this book, for instance, seems like something I've done pretty much the same way I try to get along with others; I do my work; I look at things; in short, I try to maintain my life.

So this is my first book. I'm thirty-two—I've been writing and scribbling since I was fourteen, and I've never published anything before. Just one story, a few months back, in a fiction journal, but this was a sort of anticipatory move, meaning, the book was already in the works. All told, that makes eighteen years of writing and not publishing. Now that I think about it, that's a pretty long time, especially since I've always been around people devoted to writing: by "devoted," I mean they believed that writing—their writing—was an important part of their life. A few years ago I also helped, very marginally, with a journal, a nice journal, though I can't take any credit for that, and this journal helped its founders get some notice and gradually make connections with fairly established writers, with very serious journals, with important publishers. Of these guys, a few have achieved what I'm just doing now, that is, "the book," others are getting close, and the rest are all publishing fairly regularly in the right journals. I say this to point out that even if all this was going on in a provincial city, this isn't a matter of being particularly provincial, in the worst sense. I, on the other hand, never published a thing. Not that I wasn't writing. I wrote all the stories in this book in the last year or two, but the truth is, I've pretty much always written: poems, little stories, even a tragedy in verse. There were always opportunities to publish: in the journal I mentioned or in other small journals, anthologies, etc. But

I never did. Truth is, I'm a little uncomfortable thinking about that time (some four or five years back). All these things were happening around me, but nothing seemed to be happening *to* me, and I have to tell you all now that I understood very little about what was going on back then. And so I'm kind of sorry I ever mentioned this journal and these guys, my friends: because during those years they were doing something crucial for themselves, and the right thing would be to remember that time by, well, let's say by celebrating it properly. But I can't. Back then, I just wanted to be there to help, not "to learn" or something along those lines, but to watch others live. All I wanted, for myself, was to retreat, stay hidden. Not that what I wrote stayed in a drawer. I sent out photocopies, ten, fifteen copies, to those closest to me, but hardly anyone else. I think someone said I was a flirt—that I was just playing at being the poet and didn't want to put myself to the test of publishing. But in my defense, I don't think what I was writing was all that great.

When, thanks to the journal I mentioned, my friends started connecting with other journals, with established writers, with publishing houses that were small but still important, I always hung back. There were readings I skipped, people I avoided meeting. For a while, we were inviting writers here for panels and readings, and I'd stay as far back in the audience as I could, in the back row, and I wouldn't attend the dinners. My readers were family members, a few friends, those closest to me. Sometimes I felt like a character from one of Achille Campanile's stories, the famous Gambardella. This Gambardella, Campanile tells us, was quite famous: but only among a few close friends. It was a bit like that for me. Not that these "close friends" didn't praise me, encourage me, support me. What they saw in me, I couldn't say. When I reread what I wrote back then, it all seems pretty pointless, and the truth is, I'm a little worried that a few months or years down the line, the stories in this book will feel the exact same way.

I knew all this bending over backwards my friends were doing for me made some sense, had some value, some effect. Just maybe not for me. It really felt like I was different from the others. Something was missing. Confidence—or better—the ability to acknowledge things: to tell myself and others, "I made this, and it's beautiful." I lacked this, and what goes with it: the drive to publish. Of course all I wanted was to publish. I wanted it so much I couldn't bear going through all the regular channels my friends were so doggedly pursuing: their own little journal; their first contacts; first publications in other journals; first book with a tiny obscure press, helping out with the costs; the three-line reviews; and so on. I just wanted to step outside my door one fine day and run into an editor who told me: come by tomorrow, and we'll do a book—you're really great. Someone might say that's exactly what happened. I skipped going through the regular channels. Thinking about it now, though, I have to say this feels more like I lost out in the end. I'm facing something important—something dangerous, life-changing—and I'm about as prepared as I was fifteen years back. I haven't made my bones yet, and now I have to use them.

Being around writers, pseudo-writers, wannabe-writers—smaller cities are chock-full of them—I've come across quite a few that I've tended to call "the nut-jobs." Still do. This type puts publishing above everything else, has turned it into a fetish. And of all those people so rabid about publishing, I haven't met a single one whose writing's any good. When I worked in Venice, we'd go for a sandwich on break at a coffee bar in Campo San Barnaba, and there was this little old lady, in her sixties, tiny, badly dressed, wispy gray hair, who'd wander around with a few copies of her long-dead husband's treatise on Everything in a plastic bag. She was selling it for five-thousand lire, and she'd tell everyone the story of this book, how publishing it destroyed her husband (the book was enormous, too), because he thought it would bring joy to everyone, universal joy. But all they wound up with was a house full of books. Sometimes she said her husband died of sorrow. Other times she hinted that someone wanted to hurt him, was out to get him. I have to admit I bought a copy and spent a few nights trying to figure out what was going on inside that man's head, what drove him so hard. The book was illegible, incomprehensible, even the typography was crazy, with half the words in cursive and bold-face and oddly spaced and in single and double quotes: so half the words, then, were supposed to mean something beyond their normal meaning, something modified and indefinable, which you could only guess at. That book represented a closed universe, and all you could really make out was how unbelievably lonely this man must have been. I think about how much pain it must have taken for someone to distance himself from the world like that, and how much hope this man, in his madness, had pinned on his book, like a spell to break his loneliness.

And I could also feel it, deep inside me: I was too much like the nut-jobs. I'm not talking about some obvious, superficial likeness, but something real. This philosopher with his treatise is an extreme example, but I've met doctors, lawyers, professors, very serious professionals completely taken over by this madness. Think of all the publishers making a living off them, Lalli, Joppolo, and that magazine now, *Write to Publish*. I've even learned that doctor-writers have their very own association, complete with conferences, publications, and everything, structured along the same lines as the endocrinologists' association or conferences for cardiovascular surgery.

If you're not familiar with the kind of publisher I mean, let's just say that Umberto Eco, in his opening to *Foucault's Pendulum*, is describing something very real. These people have two great obsessions: themselves and how others judge them. It's the same for me. When I sit down in front of a keyboard and start to write, I truly believe in what I'm doing. But when, a short time later, I reread what

I just wrote, I'm truly afraid. Here's why: because even if I don't think I can change or cut a single word, I also can't imagine some stranger enjoying what I wrote.

I once attended a reading by a group of women writers. They were all respectable women—I happened to be there because an ex-classmate's mother was the organizer and ran a few hotels at the Abano hot springs, very luxurious places, full of Germans. The reading was held in one of these hotels, in the main hall all done in rococo style, with white, gold, and pale-green stucco and late eighteenth-century-style furniture, rugs. There were maybe fifty women in the group. They were dressed up for the occasion. They read one, maybe two or three poems each. After every poem the room burst into applause. I saw tears of real emotion. Not one of those poems was remotely tolerable: they were all awful, and fake. I found this unnerving; it warranted some kind of explanation, but there wasn't any. These women were in complete solidarity with one another. I could never be part of such a group—I could never clap for an ugly poem. I'm not passing any judgment here—there are times to show your gratitude. But here, after these poems full of pain and nihilism, clapping, quite frankly, seemed almost uncivil. If I read a poem in public and the people burst out clapping afterward, I think I'd openly rebel. Maybe I'd scream, tell them: "You idiots—don't clap your hands like you're at the circus. I didn't just put on a show. I've expressed something here, a part of me. I've made myself vulnerable. I don't want some inarticulate response like clapping. I want silence. I want you to think about what I've read, mull it over." That's what I'd say, something like that.

At these readings—I didn't just go to the one, meaning, I kind of went looking for them, I'd go just to feel disgusted—there'd often be university professors at these things who'd analyze the poems after they were read, their praise full of erudition. Truth be told, I always thought these professors must be getting paid to do this, or maybe they were under some kind of social obligation, I don't know. But they couldn't have been serious. Maybe they did it just to get the chance to stand in front of an audience and savor what it was like to feel completely needed. The only thing I felt for these people was contempt.

Of course this was plain jealousy. You might say I was about as unfit for a social life as these people were for literature. By unfit I mean: inept. I knew there wasn't much difference between these people and me. We, the women of this group and I, were just on different social levels. Obviously, I was also jealous over this.

By "social levels," I don't mean richer or poorer. I grew up in a family that was anything but poor, though we were very isolated. We always lived much more modestly than we needed to. When I was a child I didn't understand this; I truly believed my family was much poorer than the families of my little friends and classmates. I always felt I was physically, materially inferior. My friends were allowed things I could never imagine. They had this capacity to get what they wanted, which I didn't have. I used to think that because I was poor, the right thing to do was to distance myself from what I wanted. When I grew older and realized I wasn't actually poor, I still felt inferior. I lived near others with limited intellectual and material means, yet they still lived much better than me. I felt I'd been raised to make only partial use of my resources and skills. What was left unused, I needed to conserve, for some future goal, of course. What that goal might be, I couldn't say. I still can't. I think my parents suffered a great deal from the privations they experienced during the war, and so they protected themselves, reserved their resources and skills, afraid there'd come another time of hunger and danger. My parents were teenagers during the war. My own upbringing couldn't have been better. I believe each of us has to do what we can to preserve our own existence, according to our own convictions of what we need in order to be. And so this is also why, for many years, I never wanted to expose myself to publishing.

But here I am, all the same, with this book in my hand. There's my name on the cover. It wasn't my idea to give this talk in this city where I've been living the past twenty-three years. The publisher thought it would be a great opportunity, and to tell the truth, I couldn't come up with a good reason not to. They told me that when the common reader reads a book, he thinks he's dealing with a real person. Then they told me the common reader's more inclined to buy the book when he thinks he's got something in common with the author: in this case, a city. Finally, they told me the common reader enjoys his recently purchased book more after he gets the chance to find out if the author's dark-haired or blond, good-tempered or bad, single or married, that sort of thing. So here I am, for all to see. This morning, I spoke with a nice kid from the city paper. He called yesterday and explained that to make the paper's deadline, we'd be better off meeting this morning than here in the bookstore. Five o'clock is too late, as far as a paper is concerned, for anything other than crime or headline news. This young guy had read the entire book, very carefully, you could tell. He'd almost destroyed it, pored over it, underlined everywhere, dog-eared the pages. He'd practically memorized it. He kept pounding me with questions that I tried not to answer. We played hide-and-seek for a time; then he said: "Listen, let's stop with the games. You've got a responsibility with this book. If you didn't want to get noticed, you shouldn't have published it. Or you could have published it and then moved to New Zealand. Or not even that far—there are lots of ways to keep your privacy. But you put your home address on the inside cover. And here it is—a Saturday evening—and you've got this fancy presentation in the largest bookstore downtown, with a reception and everything. Come on—be reasonable. Loosen up some."

Well, I want you to know this boy's little speech wasn't at all inappropriate. He wasn't trying to offend me in the least. He just thought I was shy and was trying to get me talking. I'd have done the same thing myself. There are writers who've managed to maintain a state of almost complete privacy. And then there are criminals who are extremely well known: we know all the robberies they've ever committed, they have identikits, they show up on bank-security footage. And yet we still don't know who they are: their names, exact ages, addresses—the details you automatically put down, for instance, when you're filling something out, some form. "I, the undersigned, Mr. So-and-So, place of birth, current residence," etc. By definition, a criminal is a public, if mysterious, personality. I realize that how I wanted to present myself on the jacket flap wasn't at all like the normal bio: I didn't want to include anything about myself except my personal data: name, age, home address. Anyone can come find me. But that's not an open invitation. I'm not looking to have a house full of intruders. I do want to say, though, if a person reads my book and wants to have some private contact with me, then he physically can. By doing this, meaning, by putting my home address on the jacket flap, I thought I was making it clear that when it came to my relationship with the public, I very much wanted to be left alone. I realize this is somewhat paradoxical, but believe me, I only realize this *now*. The person who hides might be someone who wants to be looked for or at least wants to pique other people's interest. This person also wants (secretly wants) to listen in on what others have to say about him. Like children hiding under the table to hear the grown-ups talking. I don't hide— I've never hidden in my life. Physically, I mean.

A few months back, at the start of the downward path that led to my agreeing to the production of this book, I got a call from a literary agent. He'd read something of mine that he thought was good; he'd found out someone had taken an interest in me (the editing world's a sieve, I remember thinking); in short, he was doing his job. He thought I was young—younger than I am, by the way—and inexperienced, and he wanted to offer me the benefit of his professional expertise. We had a very pleasant conversation. This man seemed truly kind, sensible, capable. At one point, he asked me what I did for a living. I told him: I'm the deliveryman for a science and technical bookstore. (Note: not this bookstore.) He said: "Now that would be something funny to stick on a book jacket." Not that I was offended. I'm very well aware that writers in this Country are generally men of letters, academics, or well-known journalists. But try telling Luigi di Ruscio that his job working in an Oslo factory is something funny.

For me, being a deliveryman is something vital. Maybe, if I think about it, there's also something decadently romantic (an old-fashioned flouting of social conventions) and childish about this, that this is how I make my living. I've had other jobs: for years, I even worked for a trade union, in their press office. I was quite willing to do the work; I was good at it. One day, I realized that what I was really good at was being obedient. No one believed in the ideals and objectives of the union more than I did, and of course it was up to me to promote these ideals. My obedience wasn't even obedience: it was complete identification, like a fetus identifying with the body of its mother. In the end, I decided I needed to find a job that still might require my obedience, but just over small things, on an everyday scale: unfair, but bearable; an existence that wasn't "happy, no, but safe," as Leopardi has the mummies sing about themselves in Dr. Frederik Ruysch's lab.

Just a few days ago, a boy wrote me from Brussels where he produces this strange Franco-Belgian-Italian journal, very grim, a touch *Métal Hurlant*, a touch Edgar Allen Poe. He went on for seven pages about this idea of his, the "rebel I"; he spoke of rebellion like it was a moral duty, even if he was talking about rebelling against pretty much every moral code; and to him this "rebel I" was a very strong I who'd be a "nonconformist" no matter what and would always find the necessary space to lead a "life of liberty" and would always go against the current, or else harness that current to suit his needs; and so on. This "rebellion of the I," according to this boy, had to be initiated by the group or maybe even by the masses, because the isolated "rebel" is scary, revolting, comes off crazy, winds up marginalized—or even worse—gets sucked back into "the system" and annulled. Now, on a regular basis and in the most ordinary of ways, I get to experience not counting for much. Even so, my "I" (sorry to refer to myself this way, like a thing, but I've been sucked into a language that isn't mine—trying to escape someone else's language, I've been snagged by it, and it's not pretty)—well, in short, I'm no "rebel." I've had to endure being subjected in so many ways to so many things that I've reached the point by now where, even if I want just the opposite, I'm basically, entirely, a "subject." I saw many young people trying to rebel, but those were very different times when, in my opinion, the call for revolution came as the new heirs were being selected to the ruling class. Some of these kids actually died; many others lost or used up all their passion for life (now gone for good) on their failed revolution; others passed the test and went on to be deemed worthy to pass over, so to speak, to the side of the selectors.

For my part, I don't think it's a good idea to take on a much stronger enemy. I prefer protecting my life, keeping everything inside. Whenever I try explaining this to someone, I'm told my thoughts are inhuman. Even my Catholic friends don't approve.

I've just made this big abstract speech, which I regret. What I should have been discussing was this phone call I got from an ex-friend, someone I hadn't seen for many years and didn't want to see, and that this friend called to say he'd read a review of my book in the paper, and then when this friend came to my home that same night to get my autograph on my book that he'd just bought (but naturally hadn't read), what I should have told this friend was: go away—I don't want to see you. Instead, I was polite; caught up in the moment, I was even happy to sign my book, and I wrote: "With the same fondness as always." Which, thinking about it, really means: "With no fondness whatsoever." I'm not trying to say I hate the people who read my book. Far from it—I'm very happy you're all here, and that you're willing to sit through this little chat of mine that's a tad incoherent, I know, and even a little offensive. The journalist from this morning made me happy, too. His questions were nice and simple: how did I get the idea for the book, what was it like to publish, what were my future plans.

In a way, I was coerced into writing this book. I'd put together a very small journal, maybe a hundred copies, with this friend of mine from Rome, a woman who wrote really beautiful poetry. The journal included some of my young friend's poems, and this small timid story of mine. I say "timid" because the story was really about someone hiding. This idea for a mini-journal, what started all this, had just sort of popped up on its own a few months before. This friend and I had been writing back and forth for years, sending each other stories, poems, ideas for movies, that sort of thing. But mostly, through our constant letters, we'd developed a friendship. I'm not sure I can say what a friendship is exactly, but I'm sure that's what she and I had. In short, with her in Rome, the center of the universe, and me in the provinces, we still both felt equally isolated, with no people around who shared our interests. Just to make things clear—I wasn't actually alone. For my part, I'd pretty much chosen to isolate myself these last few years, honestly, after spending too much time with too many people in too many unclear, exploitive relationships. Just dealing with others had become too much like work—a hassle. So I'd gone into hiding: I could do this, because there were people I really knew I could count on, a few people who were absolutely safe: the girl I mentioned;

a friend here in the city; another who's always traveling, one day she's far away, the next she's knocking at my door . . . you might say these people saw the world for me. Well, this girl and I decided we wanted to expand our correspondence, find new friends, people "like us," as she said. In one of her letters, this girl used an image I really liked: putting this little journal together was like jazz on the radio at night, when hardly anyone is listening, maybe at times, even no one's listening, but the music's playing all the same, the radio waves are traveling along through the night, embracing the world. I myself thought of something more banal: a message in a bottle.

So we put together a mailing list that included a small number of ideal readers and then the usual addresses, journals, some academics, important writers. I couldn't have guessed what would happen next. From my point of view, it was almost a mistake. And I'm still stunned by it. Since the journal was very small, with only a limited number of copies (very basic, just photocopies), I sent it out in pretty much any order I pleased. The first person to contact me, at home, was the very first person I sent the journal to, along with my sheepish little cover letter. And thanks to this person, my story from this little photocopied journal wound up reprinted in the trade magazine of a large publishing house. And now here's the book.

I agreed right away to having my story reprinted, with an enthusiasm that wasn't natural for me—and it's something I've regretted ever since. As for the book, I've been caught up in one phrase especially: "This isn't just your book—it's everybody's." I have to admit that this is true: I've experienced it a number of times myself. As a reader, of course. And I heard it on the phone from this same person who'd called me, and whom I'd only known about for a few weeks, and only through his books; and I considered his books to be mine. I really can't protest and sound reasonable. I don't mean to say I regret this book. I tell myself: it's fate. What I mean is, for me, publishing it was unnatural. Something I was forced into. "Unnatural" doesn't mean "negative," or "wrong." It means that, left to myself, I would have dropped the idea.

When I got the letter from the publisher telling me that they'd be, quote, "happy to have me among their authors," my first thought was: okay, now they've broken Pandora's vase. I truly felt my body was like a vase, and someone had struck my body so hard it cracked, and through this crack seeped my entire imagination, and my body was left empty. All my imaginings were left to wander the world, beyond my control. I could meet them on the street, meet people wearing them like puffy, translucent space suits, a sort of gray ectoplasm. And even while I thought this, I also knew this publishing offer was not only something I wanted (and had wanted all along, I might add) but that what I'd done, sending this small journal around to a group of ideal readers, etc., was exactly what I needed to do to obtain this result. And that my little story—my little timid story—was the most shamelessly seductive thing I'd ever written. Me, who can't even charm the waiter at the pizzeria. Without even realizing it, I'd done the exact right thing to obtain this particular result. And now that this result was before me, my mind and body were doing everything in their power to retreat, to return to the secrecy—practically a dungeon— where I'd preserved myself these many years. In the months that followed, I fought long and hard against my publisher friends, and I wasn't being coy, either: I was fighting for my survival. Finally, I couldn't take it anymore. Preserving my secrecy took more strength than I could muster. It was easier to live normally, in the world.

I can't really say that I'm entirely satisfied with this book as is; but I don't think I'd ever be entirely satisfied with any book of mine. There just came a point when I had to say: words, you have to go now—I don't know you anymore. You're not my children. You don't resemble me in the slightest. I don't feel a thing for you. I don't want to see you anymore. Scatter. Scat. Telling it now, I guess all this sounds pretty dramatic, but it's really what I was thinking. A year's gone by since then—no, more than a year. In the meantime, my publisher friends have broken me in some, tamed me, trained me; and so, thanks to them, I've decided to accept whatever comes in this whole business, as long as it's reasonable. But even if it's reasonable, it still makes me anxious and keeps me up at night. Standing here in front of you isn't easy. They told me I'd have to talk a while, then take any questions. I know there'll be a couple for sure, to get things rolling: I probably shouldn't say anything, but two girls from the bookstore have prepared a couple of really nice questions that I'm prepared to answer, to get things rolling. It's tragic, the moment of silence following a talk. I don't mind it myself: it's a moment to evaluate. After listening to someone for an hour, you get to decide if the person's interesting or not. The guy doing the promotion for this, who organizes these things, says he doesn't want there to be a "blob effect." They say *Blob* is one of the best things on Italian television. And the moment I start talking, I really do feel like I'm being engulfed by a blob. Like a spider feels when it leaves its hole to find an enormous lens, and behind this lens, the entomologist's enormous eye.

One of the many reasons—all of them, excuses—that I don't think the stories in this book are really publishable is that much of what's in them really happened: to me, or other people, or between me and other people. If I ever managed to write something entirely made-up, I don't think I'd regret publishing it. I could probably even "face the struggle," throw myself into the process. That story in the photocopied journal includes an incident someone saw himself in and which he asked me, in pretty harsh terms, to get rid of or at least change. I think the person suffered a great deal because of this event, even though very few people read the story with this version of the event included. I want to make something clear: almost no one, in my opinion, would have recognized the person from this passage. Later, though, I discovered that it was exactly these few lines that really made an impression on those who read them. And that's how—and I'll say it, even if it makes me sound stupid—that's how I discovered that my stories constitute the "restructuring," so to speak, of my tiny world. In my stories, the events seem determined, which wasn't true when these events occurred. In some places, I've described situations I'm still going through, but they mean something different in the stories than they do in real life. It's silly to ask which of these meanings is the real one: that could be the third meaning or the fourth. I ask myself what force compels a few real events, which can never be defined or governed, and then some imagined things, which are more defined than real events—but staying defined means always having to change—I ask myself what compels all this to hurl itself headlong into something so precise and defined as a story that has a beginning and an end. I think there must be some kind of grudge against reality in all of this.

Just by telling the story of something that happened, but changing it ever so slightly, I'm able to get my very small—my petty—revenge against this reality that's hurt me, and against my imagination for cultivating that hurt. As long as the story's there in my room, on paper or floppy disk, or only in my memory, it still gets to be imprecise or ill-defined. Seeing the story in print has a whole different effect. There's a sense of finality that I've almost never experienced in my unfinished life, and those rare times I did, it felt like a great loss. I think the relationship between things told in stories and things that actually happened is a bit like the relationship between daily events and then the transformation of these events in our dreams at night. Many have dreamed of a dear friend dying, but that doesn't mean they want it to happen. On the contrary, the dream might be some kind of exorcism. I'd like to say that my main goal in life is to return the same affection that many have for me and to at least be kind to all those others who don't have feelings for me one way or another. Maybe someone out there doesn't like me, but I doubt it. Someone did threaten me with a knife once, but it was nothing personal: he didn't hate me, he just hated the social class he thought I belonged to, had been born into. And surely this hatred comes from believing, like this person must have, that hating a particular social class can save a person's life. In the end, exchanging your own life for someone else's has a certain honor to it, at the highest level. I didn't know this guy with the knife, but he was someone who could be called a good old-fashioned "fascist thug." We were behind the high school, and it turned out he had it in for me because of my brother who was four years older and in a hostile political party. I'd only been at that school a few days, but apparently I'd already been pegged. A few years later, this guy really did kill a man. I, too, can feel it inside me, that I could harbor this kind of hate. Maybe I'm even predisposed, by nature or by upbringing, to hating this way. I'm capable of wanting violence.

I remember when my first little story was reprinted (like I said, in a large publishing house's trade journal) that they asked me for a black and white photo of myself. The journal was going to press; there wasn't much time. They phoned me on a Friday, and the photo had to be on the editor's desk by Monday morning. They told me to send it special delivery, postage due. Unfortunately I didn't have a black and white photo of myself. I took a half-hour break from the bookstore to go to the photographer's studio. The photographer told me he couldn't get me a print before Saturday at noon. There was no mail service on Saturdays. And so after the bookstore closed that Saturday, I took the train to Milan to deliver my photo in person. I'd been told the caretaker's office was open until seven. The three-hour trip to Milan was my first peaceful moment during that hectic time when so many people were just dropping into my life, various editors, literary agents, and other terrifying characters I'd never laid eyes on before. I didn't like my black and white photo. During those hours on the train, I realized I wasn't at all happy with what was going on (what others would certainly have considered my good fortune). After my pilgrimage by subway and tram, I arrived at the publishing house in the dark (it was January). The night was foggy. The publisher was located on a large, filthy street, in a half-residential, half-industrial area, really ugly. But what struck me the most was that at the top of the building—a parallelepiped structure with nothing friendly about it, but nothing negative, either, just nondescript—on the roof, I could see, from where I stood below in the dark and fog, what looked to be a lush garden. The building was six, maybe seven stories tall. After I gave the caretaker the envelope with my photo, I waited on the traffic island for the next tram, and I stood looking up at that garden. Well, imagining more than looking. There were lamps on the roof, and the garden was lit.

I'm not even sure it really was a garden: from below you could see small trees all along the edge of the roof, and it seemed like it should be a garden. I thought about the hanging gardens of Babylon, and I wondered how many centuries and millennia it's been now that hanging gardens have symbolized vast wealth and treasure. Sure, during the time of Babylon, raising water must have been a very complicated affair, while these days, practically anyone can afford a nice garden on the roof. But that night, I felt deeply offended. I'd traveled by train, hurried, come to this cold, stinking place, to bring my tiny and not so tiny offering—a photo that contained my soul—to this enormous building that housed a god who'd demanded my offering, but probably didn't even notice when he got it. The tram was arriving, and I would no doubt be returning home, diminished, dispossessed, dispirited. I'll never forget this pain. I beg you, all of you here, and I think I've finally managed to say what I had to, after all this hemming and hawing that was more from fear than anything else, because just bringing up certain things is scary, I beg you, please, try and understand my pain even a little, or at least try to accept it as something that could happen and could be true. The books I've read have taught me many things, but above all, they've taught me to preserve my life and to tuck my voice away inside my life and keep it safe—my voice, unique and private: my unique treasure and my health. I love you all.

# *Claw*

The house is small, square, and white. The roof is flat. The door, centered on the eastern side, is just a curtain with red and yellow flowers. The other sides have one square window, also centered. There's no glass in the windows, just yellowing, loosely woven cotton rags nailed to the wood like mosquito netting. The house sits on a slight rise in the middle of the plain, and anyone looking out the windows could see a long way. Down the slope from the door, there's a water pump. A leather razor strop hangs from a couple of nails in the pump's wooden handle. A small washboard rests against the pump. The house has just one room. A hundred feet to the west, there's a small shack for bodily functions. The house has a packed dirt floor. Two feet off the floor, a built-in shelf or bench runs along all four walls, interrupted only by the doorway. At the center of the room, there's a wooden table, a single chair. A few things sit on the shelf: a bowl with a set of flatware, one fork, one knife, one spoon; a covered metal bucket with a curved handle and inside, a thick soup or mash; a basin with a few soap chips and a brush; a tiny, round mirror in a metal frame, a straight-edge razor resting on the mirror; a small rectangular basket with a lid, probably for linen or clothing; a rolled-up mat. On the table, there's a white enamel pitcher with a blue rim and next to it, a slightly flared drinking glass, the bottom thick, rounded. The glass is cloudy, tinted pink. On one corner of the table, there's a canister of cigarettes with a lighter. There's a white man sitting on the chair. He has on khaki trousers and a light, collarless jacket, also khaki, but faded nearly white. He's extremely thin: those clothes were meant for someone more muscular. The man's face has a few deep lines. He doesn't have a hair on his head. He could be fifty, someone who's spent his life outdoors, but you can tell he's extremely old because he's so unnaturally thin. Another way you can tell his age: he barely moves. The man sits, facing the door, smoking. He's not looking at anything in particular, or maybe he's focused on the red and yellow curtain stirring just slightly in the breeze. The man sits rigid on the chair, left hand in his lap, right hand resting on the table, holding the cigarette, bringing it to his lips now and then. This man is Yanez, the Tiger's white brother, and this ground where his house stands is far, far from any sea, in a part of India that appears on British maps as just a milk spot scratched with a few uncertain paths that could be swallowed up at any time by thriving forests or flooding rivers.

Once a day, in the morning, a woman comes from the village (which is close, just past the line of trees to the south), and she carries the bucket of food, and once a day, in the evening, she takes the empty bucket back again. Yanez has lost his teeth and his sense of taste; the bucket holds a milky broth with small bits of meat, boiled vegetables, rice. When he started eating only from the bowl, he gave the woman his metal plate but kept the fork and knife in case a large piece of meat needed cutting. Over the years, his throat has nearly closed. The woman also brings him soap and cigarettes when he runs out and sometimes a lantern wick or a piece of flint for the lighter. Sometimes the woman brings Yanez a shirt or a pair of pants, used, but still good enough to wear. She's the only one who goes inside his house. Anyone could, but no one does. Yanez hasn't asked to see anyone in years. For what the woman gives him, Yanez gives her nothing in return. When he dies, his few belongings will clearly go to her. But no one will live in the house—no one in the village can live outside the village. Yanez only leaves the house to fill the pitcher at the pump, or to wash his few clothes or to wash himself, pouring water over his body with the soup bowl; or else he'll go to the small outhouse and relieve himself. To work the pump, Yanez must lean on the handle with all his slender might. Once a year, around the time of her wedding anniversary, the woman goes to Yanez's house with her three sons dressed in their newest, cleanest clothes. She has her sons wait by the door, she pulls back the curtain, and Yanez looks at them a while. Years ago, there were two sons, and before that, one. Yanez looks at the young man, the youth, the child, and after a while, he smiles. Then the woman drops the curtain and sends her sons away. They're healthy, handsome boys, and she's a healthy, handsome woman—she hasn't really changed with age. Yanez has never seen her husband. Years ago, Yanez went to the village by himself sometimes for supplies. The villagers knew who he was, but they never asked him any questions. The woman went to his house for the first time after they all realized no one had seen Yanez in nearly twenty days. She went once a week in the beginning; for years now, she's gone every day. The two times she was in labor, her mother-in-law took her place, but didn't go inside the house; the bucket of food she left outside the door in the morning was there by the door in the evening, empty. Yanez has given the woman two gifts: the metal plate, and on another occasion, his one book, a volume the size of his hand, three fingers thick, an English merchant vessel's log of a voyage along the eastern coast of China.

The book was filled with small pictures: strange animals, strange plants, strange buildings, men and women with narrow eyes and strange clothing. The woman's sons spent hours on boring or rainy days staring at those pictures, imagining all the strange and wonderful things he must have seen in his long, long life—this thin, silent man that people spoke of as a hero, a sea voyager, a great hunter of man and beast, brother in spirit to the Tiger. One day, before the youngest could even walk, the two older boys crept as close as they could to Yanez's house and hid in the high grass and brush and watched Yanez leave his house with a torn shirt, the basin, the brush and soap. They watched him strain to pump a little water in the basin and wash the shirt, scrubbing it on the small washboard with the soap and brush. Then Yanez pumped a little more water, rinsed the shirt, and hung it over the pump handle to dry. They were quite impressed that he'd done this women's work so easily, and they decided he could do anything at all. They never told anyone about their expedition and only admitted it to their little brother a few years later, after he swore a thousand oaths of secrecy. Their little brother knew he'd been made part of a great mystery, and he always kept his pledge.

No one knew what went on in Yanez's mind. Some of the villagers thought he'd grown old and simple. Others thought he passed the time, in the absolute silence of his house, remembering his great adventures, his friends and brothers in spirit killed by accident or men, the thousand places where his name had been pronounced with reverence or rage, friendship or fear, love or loathing. When he first arrived from an unknown place and built his isolated, small white house, even then, Yanez was silent. He only said his name. And apparently, though he'd never been to this or any other nearby village, he knew his name would be enough for whatever he needed. And he needed little. He barely spoke, only if he needed something. When he still went to the village marketplace, he barely spoke a word. For years, the rumor had been that Yanez had died, but then he arrived in the village. The village boys imagined he'd taken refuge in this safe and tranquil place to plan his next great adventure. And they waited for him to tell them that they had to choose: either the safe, boring life of the village or the brief, glorious life of the hero.

But Yanez never told them. After almost a year of talking, meeting, stalling, the most spirited boys finally gathered up their courage and went to his house. They sat by his door and waited. Yanez came out almost at once, and then the boys spoke to him, taking turns, speaking passionately, for a long time. They recalled his great adventures, told him of their own desires to win glory in this life and honor in the next. Any adventure would do—it didn't matter—it would be a glorious adventure, and they were ready for victory or defeat, because defeat at the hands of an overwhelming enemy would also bring glory on earth and honor in the heavens; they didn't know their enemy, but they weren't afraid; they'd fight anyone in his name, on the plains or in the mountains, in the rocky desert or the woods, even on the ocean that no villager had ever seen, but they knew it must be like a river with just one bank, and they weren't afraid of any river or riverbank. Yanez stood in the doorway and listened, paying close attention to each boy, fixing his eye on the one who spoke, and when they'd all said their piece, and it was clearly his turn, the minutes passed in silence, and then he bowed stiffly and stepped behind the curtain. The boys spent a long time talking about this silent answer, what it could mean. Some boys started belittling Yanez, almost mocked him. Suddenly his race mattered. Others said, "The Tiger's Claw has broken," and they were sad. It took a few years—time for the village boys to become village men—before most of them realized what Yanez's answer meant. The village was isolated, distant, and no one had ever seen an Englishman, but there still wasn't a home without something made in England that had passed through a thousand peddlers' hands. One villager, though quite suspicious, bought a sack of seeds from a bragging peddler, and it yielded thirty times the normal crop; from that year on, the children grew stronger. Some of the young men who longed to travel had gone off with peddlers to villages closer to the English, and they came back with stories of English medicines that cured almost anything and tools and machines that helped with every sort of labor. Who could resist the English when they brought such useful things? The village men wanted to consult with Yanez—he'd know everything about the English, everything good and bad—he'd fought them for so long and, really, was almost one of them, and the men wanted to know whether it was right or wrong to let the English take the village, even with fertile seeds, and strong medicines, and useful tools. The men talked a long while, but in the end they never went to Yanez—it was absurd, really—they could never keep something out that made life so much better. And then, around that time, a small caravan of peddlers arrived and brought the village its first real Englishman.

He was extremely robust, both muscular and fat, dressed all in black, with strange hair the same color you saw behind your eyelids when you closed your eyes and faced the sun. The Englishman's hair shone in the sun, seemed almost to course with blood—not the dark blood of the body—a thinner, brighter blood. The Englishman could almost speak their language, but he used strange-sounding words, and once in a while, he'd go on and on when he was really saying something fairly simple, the same way children ramble when they're first learning to talk. In the village square, the Englishman's voice thundered that he was a saint of the English god, come for their own good, to save their souls from certain death, a death they'd all soon face, he insisted, if they refused his help. The village elders met for a long time, and finally they went to the square and told the Englishman they truly didn't understand how a god, even the English god, could want or even allow men to die whom he hadn't known existed until yesterday. The English saint laughed and said he admired the village elders for their intelligence and thought their answer was especially appropriate, coming from men who had understood the best ways of thinking when considering gods; but, he added, perhaps he hadn't made himself quite clear, or the elders hadn't quite understood. He asked permission to stay a while in the village, and they agreed. For a year, all the children, women, men, and elders listened every night while the English saint told stories about his god and the people to whom his god had first appeared. The English god treated his people (who weren't English yet) like any good, stern father might treat his young son bursting with energy, both good and bad. When his people made mistakes, he punished them severely, and when they behaved, he rewarded them with his moderation. In the end, the English god wanted to teach his people a definitive lesson about the one true path, so he came down to earth as a man, yes, a real man who left his home and family when he was thirty and traveled around teaching the true path and living off the charity of others. Was he a buddha? the village asked. No, he wasn't a buddha: he was god. An avatar? Something like that. A person could get along with this English saint; his topics were interesting and sparked debate. And he knew so many other useful things: how to cure certain childhood diseases, how to get an even larger yield from English seeds. The village men thought the god of the English saint seemed just and good, though they weren't sure what to make of this idea of one god only; they might be willing to admit that he was a great god, and maybe—and this was extremely delicate—even a god more dignified and powerful than all the rest; but the English saint just kept insisting, ignoring all the evidence, that his was the one true god, and this, the village elders thought, was virtually insane; this pretense, this boundless pride was so out of character for a god who seemed so just, and kind, and good.

The English saint had been there almost a year, when much to everyone's surprise, Yanez—who hadn't left his house in years—showed up one night in the village square. He asked for the Englishman—so this was why he'd come. The English saint was astonished to see him, though Yanez didn't say his name, at least in public, and somehow no villagers had mentioned it, either, so they'd kept Yanez hidden almost a year by just not saying anything. The English saint and Yanez wanted to be alone; they shut themselves away in the room of a house, and someone spying on them through a crack in the planks said Yanez dropped to his knees before the English saint, and stayed on his knees for over an hour, almost whispering—you couldn't tell what he was saying—and the English saint listened, face attentive. You couldn't see Yanez's face, but his voice, that voice you couldn't understand, that was the voice of a crying man, a man pleading to a vast superior, even pleading to a god. After a long time, the English saint and Yanez came out from the house, the saint in front, looking as if he could scarcely believe what he'd seen with his own two eyes; behind him came Yanez, his face, as always, revealing nothing. Together they went to Yanez's house; meanwhile, in the village, people were making up stories; some were furious that Yanez had bowed down to this English saint, who maybe wasn't so saintly after all; some said if the Tiger's Claw welcomed the English saint into his home, the English saint must be good; but then others wondered if this applied to him and him alone, or whether all English saints were good (the English saint had said there were many saints like him spread all over the world, commanded by a saint of saints who lived in a very ancient city with a name that rolled beautifully off the tongue . . . Rome); and then what about the rest of the English—saint or otherwise—were they good, too? They discussed this in their homes; later, in the village square; finally, in the council of the adults and elders; and since they couldn't send a delegation to Yanez and violate his privacy, they went directly to the English saint and questioned him in the square for an entire day, the people crowded all around him. They wanted to know—and the English saint could see the change right away—they wanted to know what his intentions were, not as a saint of his god or a saint in general, but as an Englishman, if he was there on his own or if he'd been sent by other Englishmen, and if anyone else, saint or otherwise, might be coming; quite simply, they wanted to know who he was, this man who'd made Yanez kneel down and cry and plead, this man who could break the Tiger's Claw with just his presence, or better, who was so powerful, the Tiger's Claw had come down to the village of his own free will, to be broken. But their questions served no purpose. The English saint still seemed like a good man, English, yes, so different from other men, but a good man all the same.

He'd lived in the village nearly a year and told wonderful stories. He'd taught the children new ways of doing figures. He'd taught the boys and men how to make English seeds yield more. He'd taught the women how to lower a child's fever. He'd talked with the men and elders about the gods, about suffering and death. He'd laughed at births and cried at deaths, always in good measure. But he'd humiliated Yanez, they all said or thought. That isn't true, someone stood up and said: Yanez humiliated himself. Following this day of questions came a night of talk, and in the morning they all said: Yanez humiliated himself. It was a surrender, not a defeat. The English saint could stay.

After his confession, Yanez barely slept. When it grew dark, he would unroll his reed mat and lie down, but he barely slept. He'd always been a light sleeper, but he slept often. Now he lay stretched out on the mat with his eyes closed, not sleeping, and this was like sitting and staring at the curtain moving slightly in the doorway, and really, if staring at the curtain was doing nothing, staying awake with his eyes closed was doing even less. He had only a short time to live, and he wanted to live every second of it, awake. He'd made himself a bet: if the priest absolved him and kept his confession, then god existed and was good and great, because only a true, and good, and great god could do great deeds with small men; and Yanez knew that he'd committed many large sins and pardoning them was a great deed, but above all, Yanez knew that even the smallest sin was enough for damnation, so even pardoning the smallest sin, and saving a soul from damnation, was a very great deed. If the priest refused to absolve him, then he had every reason to doubt the priest's god. Yanez always knew the only one he could really count on was himself. He'd sailed a hundred seas, built and destroyed cities, been king and beggar, Portuguese and Oriental, loather and lover, friend and foe, only to find in the end that salvation comes not from what you take or lose, but from the gifts you're given and keep forever. Yanez had been given three gifts: the friendship of the pirate Sandokan, the Tiger of Malaysia; the friendship of the woman who brought him food; and, maybe, the friendship of god. Sandokan had been dead for many years now, but their friendship wasn't dead. They were friends together and friends apart, and now the great distance between them didn't matter at all. Sandokan died young and handsome, as he should—a life like that couldn't end with a frail body, a toothless mouth, a nearly closed throat, and soup trickling down your chin. This was Sandokan's gift: the lesson that all lives are different, and each ends as it should. The woman was alive and gave Yanez almost everything, asking almost nothing in return; she fed him, honored him, named her sons for him. Yanez didn't mind the woman's devotion; he knew the woman considered this to be right because of what he was: an old man who needed her. Yanez knew the woman honored him for his age and for the wisdom gained with age. That's why Yanez wanted to gain some wisdom, after so many years of life, because it was all he could give the woman in return for all her silent care. His desire for wisdom was the woman's greatest gift. The English priest came just when Yanez realized that, for all his effort, wisdom was slipping away, because, quite simply, he wasn't worthy:

he'd wanted to live a thousand lives instead of one, the right life, his life. Perhaps the priest had the power to free him from all those superfluous lives, to strip him down to the least, the poorest. This power, perhaps the priest had it, and Yanez went to the village the day he felt strong enough and weak enough to find out. Now Yanez lies stretched out on the reed mat, awake, eyes closed, and he feels like a newborn child in a basket of rags who doesn't know yet that he has arms, legs, a belly, and a back, who sees those limbs waving all around him without knowing that they're his. Yanez grabs his left hand with his right; he clasps his hands, knits his fingers; he touches his face, his neck, his chest, his belly, and his thighs; he squats, hugs his knees, caresses himself, lightly kneads his lower back; he counts his toes, touches his hard soles, the backs of his knees; he hugs his shoulders, touches his throat, the back of his neck. He struggles to his knees, as he's done only a few times by choice and as he was forced to do as a child. On his knees, almost without thinking, he prays, he gives himself.

Now he can die. When god's claw decides to strike him.

# *Trains*

When the train slips away, Mario feels he's leaving this world, the same sensation he has on sleepless nights, when he's been tossing and turning, and then, exhausted, his thoughts turn away from wanting sleep, and he's suddenly sleeping. This hard-won sleep's a dreamless sleep, or to be more precise, it's a sleep with dreams he can't remember. To Mario, the dreams you can't remember are the most important kind—they protect your vital secrets. On those nights when sleep won't come, not even with television's boredom or with a little liquor, Mario thinks his body (this same body that spares him from remembering his dreams the following morning) somehow knows there are difficult dreams ahead, dreams that need to be forgotten: and his body's afraid, and rightly so. This particular moment, right when the train's leaving, brings on a physical response, a pressure at the temples, a stiff neck. Sometimes he can read or sleep on the train; other times, he gets a headache. Mario doesn't think these headaches simply develop on their own; there's always a cause, some specific behavior: too much work, one drink too many, too little sleep. Mario's convinced he does something automatic that leads to a headache. A headache on the train, and all the way to Rome, means hours constrained to thinking without the hope of sleep or distraction. Of all the things that could happen, Mario can't imagine anything more painful than this forced company.

Mario is going to Rome, where he's been many times before. Rome is a sort of escape-city, where he can go with little fuss and find some relief. Mario isn't a great traveler; since a school trip to Paris, he hasn't had a real trip, much less a vacation, in fifteen years. But once and a while, every couple of months or so, he'll take the train on a Saturday or Sunday and head to another city: Verona, Milan, Bologna, Florence, Rome. He'll leave without a plan or program, and once he gets there, he's not really sure what to do. He'll walk around, eat at a few bars, find some stores where he thinks he can hang out a bit without being disturbed or someone trying to sell him something. He prefers bookstores. He works at a bookstore himself (as a deliveryman), so this is an excuse of sorts: he looks around other bookstores to see what they're like, to learn something. He'd like to work on the floor. He knows all the important bookstores, the ones with a certain reputation. In Florence, he likes Marzocco and Chiari; in Milan, La Remainder's in the Galleria; in Rome, Tombolini and the rare books store in the subway by the Galleria Colonna. Not necessarily beautiful bookstores, but all places where Mario can linger for a time. When his store closes in August, these quick trips of one or two days (or sometimes just an evening) can stretch out to three, four days maybe, never a week. In every city, he has his favorite *pensione*, usually an awful place, what you find on Via Fiume in Florence, or on the side streets off Via Nazionale in Rome, where you pay little and get even less: old buildings, a *pensione* on every floor, with stairs that reek, linoleum floors, paper peeling off the walls, a sink in the room. There's usually a little TV room, twenty-year-old brown vinyl armchairs, torn-up, with yellowing metal feet. Often, there's a dog. These places don't cost much, which is the point, and you can easily get a room. In Rome, if it's not high season, you can also stay at the nuns', and there everything's clean, a crucifix in every room, good *caffellatte* in the morning.

Today, Mario is headed to Rome where, perhaps, a woman is waiting for him. A few days ago, he got a letter from her saying: "I miss you" and "I wish you were here." But the letter didn't say: "Please come." So Mario's not sure if she asked him to take time off from work and go, as he's done, or if he should make his presence felt some other way, with a return letter or a small gift by mail (her letter didn't include a phone number; Mario spent two hours at the SIP phone center, trying to get her number from her address, but it was no use; she could be in a studio-apartment or a rented room, or staying with a friend or relative, who knows): Mario had considered sending her a sprig of rosemary from the bush growing in the courtyard, because rosemary symbolizes remembrance from afar, at least that's what he read in the symbolism dictionary he dug up in the bookstore a few weeks back; he also considered doing nothing at all, going nowhere, saying nothing, playing dead, not because he wanted her to make the next move (something more explicit, more direct), but really, to annihilate her short letter that seemed to be trying to resuscitate a relationship, which, by now, after such a difficult break-up and so many months of religiously avoiding one another, could only resume, in Mario's opinion, if both of them very specifically wanted it to resume, and if the stars were aligned, if they met by chance, for instance, at pre-cisely the right moment, when both he and she, miraculously, found themselves in a state of pure bliss. This isn't that time, and Mario thinks he's going to Rome because he wouldn't know what to say in a letter, except the same things he read in her letter: "I miss you" and "I wish you were here." They're nothing, Mario thinks, just words, and "I wish you were here" is something he could say to anyone when he's home alone at night, like most every night, trying to bring on sleep with some wine and television, but sleep won't come, and his longings gnaw at him, and can't be satisfied.

Mario is on the train, traveling toward a woman who, for a couple of years, he thought he loved or at least might be able to love sometime in the future; a woman he almost believed, for a few months, those last months, was the cause of all his troubles—not the woman—but the ghost of the woman, who slipped her hands under the covers to touch him while he slept, who appeared to him in a blue Fiat 500 while he was delivering books around town, but then, luckily, it was never her car: only one time it really was her car, but it was empty, parked right outside the bookstore, and Mario, who'd been out making deliveries with his little motorcycle-truck and was about to go inside, had turned around again and gone and hid in a coffee bar two blocks down, where he smoked and had an espresso and waited until the way was clear before returning to the store, even though he risked getting into trouble. No, no one asked for him, the store clerks said, no one had seen the girl, and so on. And they grinned and winked and asked him questions.

Mario defends himself with the idea that he hasn't done anything yet, that no one knows he's going to Rome; he even called his mother and told her (to muddy the waters) that he was staying in the mountains for a week, and he told his colleagues the same; he could even call from Rome and say he was taking long walks, that it was beautiful up here in springtime, partly because no one was around, that it was chilly but really nice in the sun—he really felt like dropping everything and moving to a cabin and just spending his days chopping wood. Coming up with a story is no problem. In Rome, though, Mario can go find this woman, or not. He hasn't compromised a thing. He can even send her a postcard of Rome, from Rome, and then turn around and go home, as if to say: I came as close as I physically could, but with any real contact, we'd both get burned: you miss me, I miss you, but that can't be helped; we'll just have to keep on missing each other. Mario thinks about what might happen if they ran into each other when he got to Rome: he could say he didn't get her letter, or that he did get it, but he was planning on visiting Rome anyway, for other reasons, or because he was longing for Rome, the city itself.

Mario imagines himself saying: "Just because you're here doesn't mean I can't come. Rome's not forbidden. You know—I've told you before—I think it's beautiful here: I could almost stay. You know I even tried to find a job and apartment here—we dreamed of living here together." And no doubt she would answer that this was his dream, not hers: she'd only thought of living with him the one time, the one precise moment, and that time, he was the one who pulled away. And she'd be right, of course, because that's exactly what happened: they had so many dreams, in those two years, but they were dreaming on their own, and their timing was always off. And he, Mario, never knew what her dreams were; she was like a box sealed shut, each side perfectly smooth: even so, Mario tried again and again to adapt to what he thought her dreams and desires and needs might be; and those times his guesses seemed absolutely inspired, so inspired that he threw himself into action, full of passion and energy, giving it his all, every time, what he thought were her dreams turned out to be his instead, and it might be a matter of minutes or months, but the job was already done: another gray layer between two people, thick, like sickening smoke, keeping them apart, playing on their senses, blinding them, turning their voices dull, flat: every effort meaningless, cruel, exhausting.

So I guess, Mario is thinking on the train, I guess I'll never learn. I'm only going because I'm missing something, but I don't know what that something is. I say I miss a woman, but I don't know who that woman is. I'm like a private investigator in some cut-rate b-movie, tailing someone I've never even been able to talk to. We've suffered so much, each of us on our own, each of us on account of the other. I'm responsible for so much of her pain, and a thousand voices keep telling me: turn around, turn around. But here I am, on my way, thinking, if she's staying in a hotel or has a little place, we could sleep together, but if she's at a convent or with a friend or relatives, it'll be harder. That I'm having these thoughts at all, that this is what I want, means I should keep my distance. The letter she sent doesn't mean anything, was just a moment, who knows how much she regretted it after, maybe right after. If she gave in briefly, the time it takes to scribble ten words on a piece of paper and mail it off, I can't turn her one weak moment into something huge, like this trip. All she did was let me know she misses me, and truthfully I don't know what she's missing, what I've got, or what she needs in this life or thinks she needs. I don't even know if she misses me all that much, if it's me she's missing or what she'd like from me, if it's something she really needs or something she can stand. Every time I thought she needed me, I was useless, or too much. Every time I turned away, she needed me, longed for me.

Mario shifts in his seat, trying to get comfortable. He tries lying down, since the seat beside him is empty, but the pressure on his temples grows unbearable; there's a roaring in his head of too much blood. His neck is stiff and there's no measure that can change this; the muscles in his neck have all grown deaf, unresponsive from the strain: this deafness is spreading to his shoulder blades, his lower back. If he sits up straight and rests his head against the seat, he can feel all the vibrations of the train that seem to be converging at the center of his brain, almost a tugging, like his brain is hooked, and the fisherman is pulling, tugging.

Trying to escape his headache, Mario starts thinking of some of their happier or at least more bearable times, hoping to find some comfort, gain some courage. Or else trick himself, he thinks. It was maybe a year ago, late June or early July, when he followed her up to the roof-top terrace of her building. It was evening, dark already; she'd done some laundry and had to hang her clothes to dry. The air was cool up there, fragrant. That morning, there'd been a drizzling rain that washed the city clean. The terrace was five floors up, fairly high for that neighborhood. You could smell the trees. Mario hadn't been on a roof terrace or seen the city from above in years. At ground level, the city's a terrible thing: all you see is the street ahead and the street behind. Mario, making his deliveries, had learned the city well, but when he imagined the city as a whole, it was never from above; it was just a set of routes from point to point, like tunnels. Or else if he thought about the topographic map he kept in his motorcycle-truck, it was a drawn-up, abstract idea. But from the terrace, the city and all the good smells, the lights coming from the homes (from the kitchens, bathrooms, bedrooms, televisions, and with the lights of the bicycles and scooters—there didn't seem to be any cars), the softened noises of the cool evening, the dark mysterious specks of trees—all of this—made the city seem like something human. And so this terrace wasn't just a flat, square space: it had that interesting form of things not bound by aesthetics: asymmetrical; on the one side, a canopy for hanging laundry in the rain; chimney stacks; a narrow walkway for access to some prefab sheds, added later as an attic space; absurd stairways here and there; rain gutters; various corners and low walls: a perfect place for hide-and-seek, for making yourself a little burrow, for secret places, hideouts. In their secret places, children collect rare things, marvelous things, things that are theirs alone, and private: in their secret places, children hide their heart, knowing, if the place is truly secret, no matter what occurs, they can always retrieve their heart, touch it, feel it beating, caress it, tell it stories, cry with it, love it. These were Mario's thoughts while he explored the terrace, and then he joined her under the canopy where she'd finished hanging her wash: and there, to the fresh smell of laundry soap and softener, he hugged her and told her how he felt, and he started telling her about when he was a boy living in a house in a small town by the sea and their terrace that seemed enormous, where they stored old things: a pile of wooden fruit crates, plastic tubs, old green curtains once used to shade the terrace from the summer sun. Mario and his brother made a kind of pathway of the crates out there, setting them on their sides and then draping the curtains over top, creating a dark maze they'd crawl through, searching, hunting each other. The black and white tiles were warm from the sun; it was hot in there, and the heavy curtains smelled damp and dusty, a little moldy. In those tunnels, Mario was an animal, alert to his animal enemy, to his brother's every move, and he was frightened, he'd been caught and killed a hundred times, and a hundred times he'd caught and joyfully slaughtered his brother. Mario spoke of all this, not stopping, almost in a daze, while she listened to him, their arms around each other, thighs touching, chests apart, looking at each other, rocking slightly. Then they were quiet, then Mario hurried away, practically fleeing, terrified. And this, Mario is thinking on the train, this was probably our finest moment, this memory that's mainly a memory of loss and pain.

Suddenly Mario can't stand being on the train another minute. He gets up, goes out to the corridor, heads to the bathroom, paces back and forth, smokes a cigarette. His headache is bad; he tries splashing some water on his forehead, but the water he pumps into the sink with the foot pedal isn't warm or cold and provides no comfort whatsoever. He knows why he always travels by train: because there's no stopping a train once it leaves—you reach your destination no matter what; because when a trip takes five hours, those five hours have to go by, and nothing else can happen. You're outside the world, in a separate world where time goes by in a different way and, above all, where it's not dangerous. For Mario, a Sunday at home with nothing to do is painful. In those few square meters where he lives, everything is hostile. He has two small rooms, a closet-sized kitchen, a bathroom. When he moved in, he tried making the place tolerable, paying close attention to the furniture he chose, taking more than a year to finish, because he wanted his deepest, most profound feelings, the ones he was barely aware of, to guide him in his choices. Even so, there are days when it feels like the table, couch, bed quilt, and rug all want to hate him. And on these days, he takes a train and goes.

Mario can't stand his thoughts any longer, would like to erase them all. He decides, desperately, that his thoughts don't exist: all he wants is to make love to a woman, and this woman he's traveling toward is the only one available. He hasn't seen anyone for months, he's been shut-up at home and hasn't tried in any way to fill the hole that's stayed with him, if anything he's made the hole deeper, wider: it takes up the entire apartment now, the city, everything he knows. He can't come up with one thought that's not inside this enormous hole and trembling with cold. Mario's shivering; he huddles in his seat, knees wedged against the armrest, hands between his legs, feet on the heating grate; he pulls his coat over himself like a blanket. The cold cuts at his neck. His hands ache, are frozen. It was seven in the morning when he left, and the day looked promising, like it might be clear, as clear as a mid-April day can be, from one spring rain to the next. The train window is wet with rain; at times, with the train going in and out of the tunnels, he sees gray sky and the bare, yellow Apennines. Bologna's past; his last chance to end this trip is Florence, they'll reach Florence in an hour, another hour of painful thoughts.

This train's deserted, Mario thinks. It doesn't even feel like a real train. Earlier in the corridor, he hadn't seen anyone in the other compartments; only two compartments had their curtains drawn, so maybe someone was sleeping inside, the train was coming from

Vienna, so maybe some German kids. The conductor had gone by, had suddenly, miraculously, been standing in front of him. Mario, all his muscles tight, mouth frozen, couldn't even say hello, just held out his ticket without a word, took it back. Before Florence, another would come by, another between Florence and Rome. Mario listens to the train, tries to fill his head with the sound, to sway along to it. This steady sound is more like countless distant sounds, all of them different, unrelated, unable to come together with any order or rhythm. The tunnels are scary; out the window he sees a wavering white line along the wall, going up and down, up and down, too quickly, too long, his eyes are dancing.

After a very long tunnel, the train emerges into sunshine, into a small valley where the rain seems to have just ended, the air's so clear, the grass so bright. Mario steps out into the corridor again. A flock of sheep goes by. Two more tunnels, very short, then a long curve down, and you can see the plain to the far, far horizon. Mario looks out, squints at the sudden light. From one of the curtained-off compartments, a boy emerges, huge, German no doubt, with his scraggly blond hair and beard, a red T-shirt, some kind of bandanna around his neck, purplish-gray sweat pants, a black plastic fanny pack, huge dirty blue and white sneakers. The boy stretches, looks out the window, arches, kneads his lower back. He heads for the bathroom, and Mario, leaning against the window to let him through, can smell him: he smells of sleep, sweat, travel. Mario watches the boy—his wide back—moving toward the bathroom, the boy seems wobbly, his legs unsteady with sleep and the rocking train as it rounds one curve, then another, rushing down to the plain. His wide back, his narrow waist, his agile legs though still a little numb. A girl steps out from the compartment; she's wearing a yellow T-shirt and red shorts, and she's very pale, a little chubby, with heavy, bulging breasts, her reddish hair pulled back in a ponytail. She slides down the window and, closing her eyes, sticks her face out, cold air flooding the corridor. Mario starts to shiver, but the cold air feels good; it smells of grass and rain. The girl pulls the window up halfway, leans against the opposite wall, and lights a cigarette. She has straight hips, heavy thighs.

Mario retreats back to his own compartment; he tries skimming the newspapers he bought at the station before he left. Any paper will do. His fingers are stained with ink; his fingers smell, burn slightly; he goes to wash his hands and hopes he won't run into anyone. He doesn't run into anyone. He sets the newspapers aside, watches the Tuscan landscape going by, feels nothing, falls asleep. When he wakes up, Florence is already behind him, and he didn't even notice. His left leg's gone to sleep. He tries to think but can't—his thoughts have gone to pieces—if he hadn't fallen asleep, he'd have gotten off, walked around Florence, or taken the next train home—it's sleep that trapped him, trapped him while he was trying to escape his thoughts, thoughts he should have just accepted and endured. Mario hates that he's so weak—he shouldn't have started on this trip at all, and he wonders if he can do it, if he can get to Rome and leave, turn away from the cause of his evil, from repeating his mistakes.

# *Glass*

Two years ago, we called someone out to replace the windowpanes on the small, enclosed porch that was there when we moved in, twenty years ago, built onto the tiny balcony overlooking the back courtyard. It's a metal-frame porch, with windows about a half-meter square. The glass panes might have been naturally tinted gray, but they were also caked with filth. Some were broken, others cracked. Some must have been replaced already: the panes that looked the oldest had strands of wire in the glass. We wanted a porch with more light, more dignity. The balcony space is small, only one and a half by two meters, and just fits a few pots of geraniums and in the winter, some small crates of fruit and some bottles of wine. The porch worked well enough, but we decided to fix it up anyway. The man we hired didn't even try to pull out the old glass: he taped cardboard to the inside of the frames with packing tape, then hammered out the windows, spraying broken glass over the gravel below. Then he pulled off the cardboard and any glass still stuck in the frames, and he tossed all that into the courtyard, too. Then he installed the new panes. For a few days, we went out and picked through the gravel for glass shards. Then we gave up. On Sunday mornings, after a long, hot shower, I like to go out in the courtyard around ten o'clock for a cigarette, my first of the day. If it's raining, I lean back against the door, just under the balcony. Winters, I'll still go out in a T-shirt: I like the cold after a hot shower. If it's not raining, I'll take a walk by the plants and look at things. I especially like the dividing wall between our yard and the neighbor's to the right. It's just a dividing wall, and that's probably why it was thrown up without much thought, back when they built the house, after the war. It must have been a brownish-orange once, like the house, but the paint seeped into the mortar, leaving only some dirty-gray stains and a touch of blue. The sun never hits the wall: it's damp, blotchy, shaded and streaked with dark-green and silver moss. In some places, you can see swellings, blisters—popped blisters. In other places, the mortar's flaking off or crumbling. The layer beneath is yellowish, dusty. Years ago, the wall was covered in Virginia creeper that spread from the courtyard next door. I'm not sure why, but our neighbor decided he didn't want this vine anymore, so he cut it off at the base and dug up the roots. The vine shriveled up, and we finally tore it off on our side. Some of the stems took bits of mortar with them, but others stuck to the wall and are there still, thousands of tiny paw prints, like the signature of some disease. Clotheslines hang from one end of the wall. The expansion screws are old now, rusted, and under each one, there's a trail of rust creeping to the ground. I like looking at this wall, at its meticulously worked surface, and I see it as deliberate work—not a person's deliberate work—I see it as the work of things, of chance. Naturally, I can't help thinking that I'm like this wall, that I'm a worked thing, too, adorned with this same, almost endless variability. There's something I keep trying to say, that grammar won't permit, won't allow. Clearly, a person didn't do all this work, though there's definitely a purpose here, and I'm the one who's decided this purpose, because I'm really happy seeing all of this, and

I'm happy thinking the purpose was making me happy. Last Sunday, I was outside smoking, and I saw more glass shards in the gravel, so I started picking them up, tossing them in the bucket that's still in the courtyard, probably from the last time the painters came, last summer. I pick up glass fairly often, and there's plenty in the bucket already. Last Sunday, I must have found a dozen pieces. When you first look down, all you see is gravel, but there's still so much glass. You have to look closely. When you see a piece, even if it's just two steps away, you have to keep looking while you take those steps, and then you have to keep looking while you kneel and reach for it, or else it's lost. Some pieces are almost buried, or they're so dirty you don't see them right away. I like picking up shards, because whenever I want to, I know I'll be able to find some, and if they're getting harder to find, I'm also getting better at finding them, which seems like a fair tradeoff to me. Last Sunday while I was gathering shards, I started thinking that it's almost like trying to gather important memories, that you have to look for memories in something like gravel, something so indistinct from far away and so varied close up, it'll make your head spin. And sometimes you think you've found them, but take a step in their direction, they've disappeared. And I understood that this thing I thought I was doing for sheer pleasure, I'm really doing so I can imagine I'm doing something else, something that gives me the strongest feeling, but that I can't describe. I take it as a sign, and I'm extremely grateful to those things that—without my even being able to ask—have given me a tangible symbol of something I've been working on a long while. I understand now that gathering shards strengthens my soul, comforts it, helps it to see that even if the windows have shattered, they can still be recovered, piece by piece. Each shard is dear to me. And I'm glad this is the sort of work you can't finish—really, it would be extremely sad to finish, to find yourself with your soul all in one hand. I've come to think that each part of the soul is the entire soul, and that the entire soul is made up of infinite parts, like shards of glass, like gravel, like the surface of the wall.

# *Tana*

The rain began that morning. Tana was coming home from school. Thursday afternoons they had sewing class, and now on the bus, she realized this was the first day she'd left school with no light in the sky. It would go on like this for months. It was cold out, raining, and the bus, jammed with boys and girls, with students, was steaming hot. The windows were fogged up; someone had managed to pry one open, and Tana, already sweaty, was freezing. She thought: I might get sick, stay home a week. She didn't try to get out of the draft; she didn't protest. The rain hit her face, her eyes. It hadn't rained in a while and the city and air were full of dust. She felt the rain burning against her face, her eyes. The bus was incredibly noisy, but so much noise filled Tana's head that all the passengers seemed to be opening their mouths with no sound coming out; they were silently laughing. She remembered reading in the encyclopedia about a South American Indian tribe that lived surrounded by ferocious enemies; as a result, the men and women hardly ever spoke and the rare times they did was just to whisper in each other's ear; they bandaged the children's mouths until they learned the rules; they cut the hunting dogs' vocal chords with special, long, sharp knives. That way their enemies didn't hear a sound. Everyone in the village moved with extreme caution, with silent steps. They didn't build fires. Maybe, Tana thought, it wasn't even a real village: each person had a cloak, and that cloak over his head was home. Shut up in his house, the person from a distance must have looked exactly like a bare shrub, or the torn-up roots of a rotten fallen tree, or some rejected animal carcass. Something no one was interested in. To avoid any cooking smells, the animals they killed they ate raw, and they ate every last bit, down to the last bone and shred of skin, down to the last feather, not leaving even a trace behind. Maybe the tribe never gathered together; each of them wandered alone in the dense, dripping forest, wives and husbands meeting only now and then, always in different places, always on days set according to different rules. Though often, just to be safe, they didn't meet at all. Or more likely, a man wandered the forest, leaving it to luck or to the gods if he met a woman, and if he did, then she would be his wife, and if he met a man, then that man would be a friend or foe. It was her stop: Tana jumped up. At first the mass of students seemed to strain to hold her back, but then it pushed her out with more force than she expected. She stumbled onto the sidewalk, stunned. She opened her umbrella too late; rain ran down her hair and neck. There was an electric clock above the bus stop sign: the trip had taken almost an hour, not the usual twenty minutes.

Tana was shivering. Her backpack felt heavy; her arm holding the umbrella was so tired, it ached. Her clothes were ice-cold. Let's hope I get sick this time, she thought. Tonight I'll have some broth from yesterday's stewed meat, nice and hot, with bread. And I'll have a little wine to bring on a fever. I'll put on two pairs of pajamas and an extra blanket so I'll sweat a lot. I want to stay in bed a week—I want to stay in bed so long I'll think my bed's really awful from then on. Tana was walking slowly, almost blind, her umbrella over her face to protect her from the burning rain. She made no effort to avoid the puddles: good, she thought, I'll get even sicker. And I can always have as many shoes as I want. The passing cars splattered up her thighs. Her shoes had come untied; her flowered leggings were soaked; her heavy jacket stank like a wet dog. Tana took the side street; she could barely make out the traffic light at the end, only some fifty meters away. She saw the angel just as she crossed the street by the traffic light. What she really saw was a pile of feathers, a sort of ball pressed up against the lowered shutter to the grocery shop. The shop's glass front came in slightly, by a half-meter, so those feathers were at least a little protected from the rain. You could tell they were white feathers, but they were filthy with rain and mud. The mud was blackish-red and made Tana think of blood. She approached carefully, holding her open umbrella in front of her, ready to defend herself. What Tana saw was like an enormous bird, but as she circled at a slight distance, there was a very pale, helpless foot poking out from under the cover of the wings. She came forward and saw that the pile of feathers was jerking slightly, an erratic, uncontrollable tremor. She came closer and tried to speak. She didn't know what to say. She said: "What's the matter?" in more of a whisper than she liked, and at once she thought "What's the matter?" was a really stupid thing to say. But what should she say, then? She came even closer, shifted the umbrella to her left hand, stretched out her right and touched the pile of feathers; she leaned forward, closer. The pile jolted, the wing moved slightly, and underneath Tana saw some blond hair smeared with rain and dust. She tried to pull the wing aside—it resisted a little—and there was a face with closed eyes. She touched the angel's forehead, which was cold, but not freezing cold. That forehead didn't move under her touch. Once again, Tana said: "What's the matter?" but there was no answer. Then she said: "Can you get up?" and the mass of feathers answered with an uncertain shudder. That must mean no, she decided, and she closed her umbrella, slipped it through the loop on her backpack, and she lifted the angel, reaching into the feathers, raising him by the armpits. It didn't take much effort, even if her backpack threw her off balance. The angel was much bigger than she was but not that heavy. Tana tucked her shoulder under the angel's left armpit, put her right arm around the angel's waist, then shoulders, and with her left hand, she gripped his left arm. From below, she looked up at the angel's face, at his eyes, which seemed slightly open. She said: "Come on—you can do it," and they started off.

The angel kept nearly falling, but then right when they were both ready to tumble onto the flooded sidewalk, he'd take a step. Tana's condominium was the fifth one on the left, just before the levee. The street was empty. The houses had their sliding shutters down to keep out the rain. Tana announced at the intercom: "It's me," and she pushed the angel into the elevator. She leaned him up against the elevator mirror and let go. She dropped her backpack. At her floor, she helped the angel into the apartment, dragging her backpack behind her. She quickly got the angel to her room and shut the door. Her mother was shouting something from outside the door; Tana shouted back that she was soaked through, that she was changing, and then she'd take a hot bath and go to bed, she didn't feel well, didn't want anything to eat, just wanted to be left alone. When Tana shouted like that, her mother never insisted on coming in or saying what she had to say. Her mother was the only one home at this hour. Her father and Sergio nearly always came in together, at eight, and tonight they'd be even later. Tana positioned the angel on the floor, propped up against the bed. His wings were open, huge. The angel's eyes were still closed, but while she was moving him, it felt like he was trying to help. She took off her shoes and tossed her soaked jacket over the chair; she stood there thinking, then opened the shuttered wardrobe door and, standing behind it, peeled off her leggings, ankle socks, and undershirts, and tossed them on the floor; she put on her heavy blue sweater and gray sweat pants. She was searching for her slippers under the bed and heard the angel take a deep breath. He hadn't moved. Tana cracked the door open—the hall was clear—and praying no one would see, she quickly steered the angel to the nearby bathroom that she shared with her mother. She set him on the edge of the tub, his left shoulder against the wall, wings tucked in, legs facing out to keep him from falling. Without her guidance, he'd just be gripping the tub for support. His hands were very white. She didn't dare look him in the eye. The angel's head was bent down toward his chest, like someone bobbing asleep on a train. Tana turned on the hot water and started washing the angel's wings with the shower hose. The angel wasn't what she expected. He was almost what you saw in catechism pictures, but not quite. His wings weren't attached at the back, from the shoulder blades, but from the same place as the arms, though the arms rotated like human arms and the wings seemed hinged to rotate toward one another, then backward. And they weren't bird feathers: they were flesh, like very slender tongues, the skin paler and thicker than normal skin, rougher. The angel had on a sleeveless white tunic—but filthy—that came down almost to his feet, with slits up the sides to the knees. She ran the jet of warm water over his wings, scrubbing them with a sponge; she wasn't entirely sure what she was doing, but maybe he was chilled through, even suffering from hypothermia, and she had a feeling his wings were his weak spot: they were so much paler than his face or arms.

In a short time, the wings started moving, seemed to be stretching, and the tongues of flesh were rising, letting the warm water penetrate beneath; the skin below was no longer pale; it was bright pink, the web of capillaries pulsing: this didn't seem like skin; it was more like—and Tana had also read this in the encyclopedia at home—like an internal membrane. The tongues of flesh were captivating as they rose and fell, row by row, like a wave, the wings moving only slightly, as though the angel, checking to see that they still worked, was afraid to bend them any further. These wings were fascinating, almost a live thing on their own, and then seeing the pink beneath the tongues, Tana thought of her own tongue in her mouth, and she was suddenly filled with disgust, and she turned away from the wings; she raised her head to see the angel staring back at her over his shoulder, and she was afraid. The angel had red eyes. One of her classmates, Maria, had a mother with eyes like that: she was an albino with white hair and skin so transparent it was disgusting. The angel was staring at Tana, staring, his eyes steady and confident, and she didn't expect this at all; she thought he'd be afraid, shy, keep his eyes down; but he was shamelessly staring, eyes narrowed, as if to get her into better focus, with no shyness whatsoever, and no curiosity, no gratitude, either. Tana was frightened. She dropped the shower hose and ran to her room. She felt like crying; her head was spinning. What now? What now? she thought. The angel might be dangerous, cruel, she thought. With those red eyes, he might even be a demon. But then she thought how stupid it was—being afraid of an angel—and what if her mother went into the bathroom and saw him, she thought, and her stomach clenched with fear. She cracked open the bedroom door and no one was out there. She slipped into the hall; she hadn't shut the door to the bathroom all the way when she ran to her room. She peeked in: the angel was sitting with his legs in the tub, methodically washing his feet. She watched him, wondering why she'd been so afraid: there was nothing to be afraid of; it was stupid thinking the angel had to be like she'd always imagined. She watched the angel, admiring how he took care of himself; he seemed perfectly capable, and she felt disappointed—then ashamed of herself for being disappointed—of course an angel knew how to take care of himself and could wash his own feet. And Tana knew how completely wrong it would be to keep thinking the angel needed her help. She could offer her help, and she had, but she also needed to know when to stop. Feeling better, she went back to her room; she'd leave the angel alone. But she left the door partway open so he wouldn't think she was rejecting him. Her head seemed to be clearing; she felt brave and secure.

Just then, she heard her father and brother in the entranceway: when the weather was bad, they'd arranged that Tana's father always picked up Sergio. Her father worked in a shoe store and had found Sergio a job two years earlier at the same store where he'd worked years before and was still friends with the boss. He'd never come get me, Tana thought. Her father and Sergio never liked each other much, but they'd bonded since Sergio started in the same job. They were colleagues; they felt important and special. At night, the only thing they seemed to talk about was shoes; Tana couldn't stand either one of them. Sometimes she thought she should figure out a way to team up more with her mother so they could face the two males together, like women had to. But it seemed as though her mother had decided the only way to get the men to think of her at all was to serve them with absolute devotion, and that left no room for Tana. All of this came to her as she heard Sergio and her father returning home, and she realized she'd never find an ally in this apartment, or any place for an angel. They'd never even notice him, she thought. She heard her father and Sergio speaking, and she could hear that their voices were strange. She couldn't make out their words, couldn't tell what they were saying; their tone sounded sharp; they were almost shouting; but she had no idea if they were happy or upset; their voices were like a 33 LP set to play like a 45. Tana looked down the hall, and her father and Sergio were running around at high speed—just like their voices—not like people hurrying, but like characters in a revved-up film. They were racing in and out of their bedrooms, the kitchen, their bathroom, moving so fast, they jerked. They were doing what they always did when they came home at night; Sergio, always so fussy about what he wore at work, was taking off his shoes and putting on his sweat suit; they both were washing up: but it was as if they had to push themselves to do the usual things; it took an exaggerated effort; as if, Tana thought, they had to put in their whole life's effort, the effort of every single cell. Now they sounded happy, but she still couldn't understand. She stepped into the hall and came toward them. They didn't even see her. Different expressions kept flashing across their faces, across her mother's face, and Tana couldn't make out any of them. Their faces were like those claymation figures she'd seen in the bitters commercial. She went into the kitchen; the red tablecloth appeared on the table along with four plates, and she automatically sat down at her usual place. Her mother, father, and Sergio were eating in a frenzy, as though they hadn't eaten for a year. Tana sat still, dazed; at one point she felt her arm being steadily tapped, it was her mother, and she realized her mother was saying something in that new incomprehensible language, probably trying to get her to eat. But she barely had time to think this before the tablecloth vanished, her mother clearing off everything, racing, tossing the plates into the sink like a juggler tossing tennis balls or colored pins, not breaking a thing.

Tana got up from the table—she hadn't eaten—and she went back and slipped open the bathroom door: the angel, looking satisfied, was studying his feet, clean now, washed and warm, a lovely rose color. Water sparkled in his soft, blond curls. He'd managed to clean up his tunic a little. He looked more dignified and seemed very strong. Tana took comfort in this. When she opened the bathroom door all the way, the angel looked up, got to his feet, and smiled at her, not a friendly smile, she thought, more satisfied than friendly, but at least he was smiling, and she said: "You want to eat?" The angel said: "Yes," without so much as a "thank you," but he spoke so quickly that Tana thought: he's starving; and his voice sounded uncertain, still weak, without the force that seemed to fill his body and wings. Tana took the angel by the hand and led him to the kitchen. Her father and Sergio were watching TV in the living room, leaping up, constantly shifting positions on the couch, and speaking in their new shrill voices, probably about shoes; her mother was in her usual spot in the kitchen in front of the smaller TV, her chair turned so she could rest her left elbow on the table, her chin in her hand; the TV was flashing, but Tana could see it was the usual soap opera, and her mother was asleep like always, and she'd only wake up at the end when the commercials came on at a higher volume, and she'd curse about missing yet another half-episode and come up with a hundred theories about what had happened while she slept—though really, Tana thought, nothing ever happened on that soap opera: phone calls went on for hours while the old man was dying, everyone fighting over the money, with him in agony for maybe twenty episodes. Tana sat the angel down at the table; she took the small pot of broth from the fridge and started heating it up; she sliced some of the leftover bread, threw out the crumbs, and pushed the slices down into the big bowl she'd had since she was little and miraculously never broken, not even one of the handles; she emptied the grated-cheese container over the bread, then poured in the warm broth and slid the bowl toward the angel. The angel was staring at her the whole time. Tana had a cat some years back that stared at her in the same way, from a distance, but paying very close attention as she prepared its food in a small bowl. Meanwhile, her mother had woken up, turned off the TV, told her a few things in that new voice of hers which Tana didn't need to understand, and then her mother sat down in her same spot to mend some socks. She's going so fast, Tana thought, she's going to prick her finger, but her mother didn't prick her finger. And Tana tried to avoid looking at her mother, and her father, too, when he came into the kitchen for a match to light his cigarette; Tana sat facing the angel, trying to concentrate on him alone. The angel was slowly sipping the broth, taking a big spoonful, pausing quite a while, taking another; then he began to scoop up the bread at the bottom of the bowl, and she realized he was trying to get it all up at once without tearing the pieces apart.

The broth smelled nice and hot; Tana was extremely hungry, but she knew this wasn't the right time, not now. She watched the angel set the spoon on his plate and raise the bowl for the last drop. When he set the bowl down, he gave her another satisfied smile. His eyes seemed a little less red now, or maybe the red was a little less piercing and raw, as if the broth's warm vapor had dimmed his eyes, softened them. He must have been really cold, Tana thought, even on the inside. She recalled being sickly cold and how satisfying it was to wash herself warm, eat warm, wrap herself back up in wool. She asked the angel: "What's your name?" The angel said: "Roberta." Tana didn't know what to think; on the one hand, the angel had been quite comfortable saying "Roberta," as if "Roberta" was exactly the right name for an angel; she looked at the angel, at that simple, unmarked face, like the face of a child, without a trace of beard; but the tunic fell straight from the chest, and though the face was childish, it was definitely a male face, and those arms on the table were male arms (but they weren't resting on the table like arms do, Tana thought, they were more like two things the angel didn't need just then), and she'd seen the angel's feet in the bathroom and they were big, male feet. She forced herself to answer: "My name's Tana, but Tana's really short for Gaetana. I've been Tana since I was little, though, and didn't really know how to talk—" she stopped: the angel looked bored; she stopped and thought: why am I telling him this? A name is a name. He didn't ask me mine. His is Roberta; she looked at him, embarrassed, and he was staring back at her with no expression, just watching with the faintest hint of expectation—not that he wanted something, more like he was available—she didn't fully understand and just kept staring. Her family must have gone to bed, she hadn't noticed, but now she remembered that while the angel was eating, she felt something brush against her right cheek, and then her father hurried away; he kissed her every night, if she didn't shut herself up in her room first to avoid that kiss—it was so humiliating, like she was a child—but tonight she hadn't noticed, hadn't realized she'd been kissed. She led the angel back to her room, pulled her pajamas out from under her pillow, turned down the covers to her bed (which was a three-quarter bed because ever since she was a little she'd tossed so much in her sleep she kept falling on the floor, so they got her this wider bed a few years back), and she gestured to the angel that he should "make himself comfortable," though she didn't dare say a word, and then she fled to the bathroom. She studied herself in the mirror: she was still filthy, her hair smeared with dirt, her eyes tired. What little make-up she'd put on had run down her cheeks. She was shivering. In the bathtub, she washed herself thoroughly, then sank down in the hot water to warm up some more; she was also hoping the angel had settled in and gone to sleep. But then she started worrying that while she was shut up in the bathroom, the angel might take the opportunity to leave, and she splashed out of the tub, wrapped herself in a big towel, and leaned out to check: the angel was sleeping on top of the blankets, using his wings as a pillow and also to cover himself up a little. She felt calmer and went back to the bathroom, dried her hair, and slipped into her pajamas that she'd laid over the radiator to warm. The angel was fast asleep on the side of the bed closest to the wall; Tana slipped under the covers, turned off the light, closed her eyes.

Tana, eyes closed, was thinking about the angel's sex organ. She hadn't realized it, that this was what she was thinking about, until the angel said his name. Maybe he'd said it on purpose, and it wasn't even his real name. A few months ago, at the end of June, she and a group of around fifteen others, boys and girls, had taken scooters to Camin's Pit, just outside town. The sun was hot, but Tana was cold, even though she had on a light sweater and was sitting behind on the scooter and out of the wind. It only took ten minutes to get to the pit. The water was gray and still. The pit had been dug two years earlier, for the new beltway, and then no one filled it in. And so it stayed. The road was a few meters away, hidden by the line of trees. There was grass, some bushes. The pit was somewhat forbidden because apparently there were weirdoes wandering around. And sometimes drifters set up camp, but never for more than a few days. A few posted signs read, "No swimming allowed." It was filthy behind the bushes. At the height of summer, a lot of people came, and the city council sent workers in once a week to clean, even though, theoretically, no swimming was allowed. At this time of year no one came, so no one came to clean. There was also some netting around the whole area, including a small ditch, but the netting was half torn down and someone had found a couple of good places to lay boards across the ditch. The boys and girls knew that over there, all you had to do was slip behind a bush or cover yourselves up with a towel, and you could make love, and no one would say a word. One boy threw the idea out there, and then all the boys were racing not to be last, as they stripped and jumped into the water. They splashed around a bit, the water just up to their waists (it was only deep in the middle of the pit), and then they climbed up the bank of the pit, looking slightly blue and numb. They made excuses about having to dry off, and so they stood naked in front of the girls sitting on the bank. One girl was shocked and screamed and went off to sit by herself, her back to the boys. The boys stood with their hands on their hips, shivering, their genitals just at eye level. All the boys were thin and beautiful, at least Tana thought so. The boy closest to her, who went to a technical school, she'd only seen a few times before in the group. She moved over a little without getting up, so she could see better.

The boy turned slightly toward her. A patch of hair rose from his groin, thinning, disappearing toward his belly button. His chest was smooth, white, with just a few long hairs twisting around the nipples. Tana looked down at that thing dangling in the clump of dark hair. It seemed weak, strange. She raised her right hand and touched it with one finger, and she saw it jolt. She pulled her hand back; the thing was swelling. The boy shifted just a little closer. Tana held her hand out straight and slightly cupped so she could lift that thing and see the semi-hidden testicles, and she felt it rise on its own, still swelling, growing stiff, and on the tip, there was an opening in the skin, and a purple stain. Tana kept staring, amazed, at this thing in her hand, watching it change, and she felt the boy's hand from above, touching her neck, pushing down, trying to get her closer. Tana let go; she drew back, scrambled to her feet; she stood there staring back and forth at all the boys; she didn't know what to do. Then the boys put their clothes on, silently, and they all went back to the piazza. The boy Tana had touched tried to get her to climb on the back of his scooter, but she kept her distance. A few days later, he called (one of the others must have given him her number) and calmly suggested that they go out next Saturday; his parents would be gone until Sunday night. They could go to the movies and then she could come over; he'd make them some dinner and get them something to drink, some cigarettes. Tana listened, and then she hurled as many insults at him as she could, calling him every name she knew, and even some she didn't. She saw him a few more times in the piazza but always avoided him. Once while she was out, she turned around to see him laughing and talking with two other boys, and she could feel them watching her. She screamed something after him, and the boys started laughing until her friend pulled her away. They slipped into a coffee bar, and the girl said she really didn't understand Tana: she was really an idiot not to go out with him, this girl had actually tried, but he didn't give a shit, and all the other girls there told her he was really a good guy, he always paid, and he always had a rubber, and they'd have fun together. Tana, lying in bed with her eyes closed, the angel breathing beside her, remembered what she'd decided that day: that god had been especially cruel to men and women, giving them this awful reproductive system, jumbling up the organs, so those organs that gave the greatest pleasure, the parts concentrated on love, were all mixed together with the most disgusting parts; and so, ever since the pit, her vagina was disgusting to her, and she stopped touching herself, stopped masturbating, though she still felt desire—sometimes at night, a raging desire—and more disgusting still was that with this desire came the boy, standing there naked, and he was beautiful, gorgeous, whatever she touched she was touching him, and she saw the two dark stains of his nipples, and in her hand, that flesh, soft at first, then swelling, enormous, and the purple stain opened, there was a sour smell—Tana, during her nights, forced herself to look at that reddened flesh, which, if she kept imagining long enough, suddenly spurted a yellow, foul-smelling, never-ending stream of urine; she felt it gushing out, that urine, with its rotten smell, felt it wet on her body, lukewarm, revolting, she even tasted it in her mouth, and it was only then, thanks to this remedy, that the image faded, her desire grew indistinct, weaker, then almost disappeared, and Tana stopped feeling and lost herself to sleep.

Now Tana turned on the small lamp, and rolled over to look at the angel while he slept. She got to her knees on the bed. She inched forward as softly as she could. The angel's wings were slightly spread; he looked a little disheveled. He looked like someone who was sleeping so deeply, his extreme exhaustion had to wear itself out before he woke up again. His knees showed under his tunic. Tana was afraid, but she also had a thought she couldn't shake: that this was why the angel was here; this was why he'd allowed her to find him, clean him, feed him: to make her understand that he was available, that she could do whatever she wanted. Anything you could do with an angel would be okay. Tana slipped her right hand under his back, lifted him a little, and with her left hand she gingerly drew up his tunic. She laid him back down, and knelt by his knees; she hesitated, then lifted the hem. The angel's sex organ wasn't circled by hair. It looked like a child's, only larger. Tana thought it was beautiful. The flesh was very pale, like the rest of his body. His belly peacefully rose and fell with each breath. Tana, propped up on her left hand, touched the angel's belly with her right, not pulling away, running her fingers over his left thigh, between his legs, up his right thigh, onto his belly. Her fingers came near his sex organ, but she didn't dare touch it: not out of disgust, absolutely not, but out of respect. She wanted him to stay asleep. She brought her face closer to his sex organ, to see it better in the halflight; it was smooth and clean and didn't smell bad. She touched his sex organ with her lips, a small kiss, like you'd kiss a sleeping infant, kissing him without waking him. His sex organ didn't rise. Tana kept looking, kept running her fingers along the same path, never touching it. She liked doing this. After a while, she felt sleep pressing down on her, from inside her head, her legs and left arm were tired in this position, and then she covered the angel back up and looked at him. She looked him over, from head to toe, his wings and arms and fingers, and he seemed entirely beautiful. Looking at the angel, she felt no desire whatsoever, just pleasure, pleasure at touching him and giving him that very light kiss on his sex organ. And then she thought it must be very late, and she burrowed under the covers and shut her eyes tight so she'd fall fast asleep, and she dreamed that the angel was leaving, flying away. He was flying away and all along his path, below, the roofs were coming off the houses, and from the houses rose a golden light piercing the dark night sky. The next morning, Tana woke with a wonderful fever, and she was filled with tenderness and dreams and the joy of staying cuddled up in bed and phoning her school friends to come see her, to make them jealous of her good luck, a week's vacation, while outside, it was raining everywhere, and the rain was washing the world, preparing the world for winter, so lovely.

# F.

"It's all theater. When they decide to, the mafia will kill me anyway."
—Giovanni Falcone

The magistrate, alone in his room, is trying to sleep. He slouches in his chair, shuts his eyes, settles his arms on the armrests, stretches out his legs. He's extremely tired. The florescent lights are bright: in front of his closed eyes, the magistrate sees black and purple specks disappearing into two large red spots. His eyes hurt; they burn. The armchair is comfortable, but he can't find the right position. The magistrate sinks down, down some more, but now he's too hunched over, and it hurts at the base of his spine. He sits up, but after a few minutes, the circulation to his thighs is cut off, and his legs start to fall asleep. He turns his head to the right, to the left, the cool leather soothing his temples, the two red spots less pressing, but this puts a strain on his neck and makes it hard to breathe. He realizes he's clenching the armrests and tries to open his hands, but now his arms don't feel secure; they might drop to the floor. The magistrate jolts to—he's been sleeping a few seconds, a few minutes—his left arm slipped sideways off the armrest and woke him. His left hand tingles. The light's painful, and the magistrate tries to cover his eyes with his left hand, but the hand is heavy, still asleep. He checks his watch: only a few minutes since the last time he checked. He laces his fingers across his stomach, lets his head drop forward, feels his neck grow stiff, his beard stubble scraping. He tries to stay still, hoping to fall asleep, though he's completely uncomfortable. The light can't be turned off. There's no natural light: the room's two windows were bricked up months ago and now a built-in safe almost blocks one of these windows entirely. The brickwork's bare, red brick with gray-mortar stripes. The magistrate, who can't sleep, listens to the sounds coming from his quarters that are isolated from the rest of the building. There's the hum of the small generator for his separate power system. And someone walking down the hall. Now and then a phone rings, but he can't hear any voices. There are no doors to the rooms in his quarters: the guardian angels took them, and now all that's left are the two fire doors to the single entrance. This way, whoever's patrolling the hall can see into every room. In the magistrate's room, in the furthest corner from the door, a convex mirror hangs two meters off the floor so you can also see down the hallway. It's the same in all the rooms. The magistrate, eyes closed, is completely still now, maybe he's been sleeping a few minutes. Arcangelo has entered the room; he's standing by the table, looking at the sleeping magistrate. Arcangelo is standing there looking at the magistrate, looking at him, listening to the magistrate's breathing as if, by the rhythm of this breathing, he might figure out what kind of sleep this is: an exhausted sleep or one from unbearable tension or tension soon to be relieved. A restful sleep that puts your thoughts in order, or one that makes you feel bad after, muddle-headed. Slowly, Arcangelo draws his lips in, and almost whispering, he says: *bang.* The magistrate flinches, gripping the armrests, wide-eyed, sees Arcangelo. Then he slumps back, sprawled in the chair.

"Arcangelo, you idiot, you scared me."

"Scared's my job, Mr. Prosecutor, not yours. You trying to steal my job?"

The magistrate can't stand it when Arcangelo talks this way, part hired gun, part lone avenger. Still, the magistrate knows what he, Arcangelo, means when he talks this way and considering everything, Arcangelo's right. He means: security's my job, the inquest is yours; try your hardest not to worry about security, because I'm here, and that's what I'm breaking my back over the whole damned day. The magistrate thinks: this is all I can do, entrust my life to this man. If it were up to me, I'd be much worse off. Arcangelo sits down at the table opposite the magistrate, steadily staring him in the face and asks, "Are you all right?," sounding almost casual as he pulls a scrap of paper and a pencil from his right pocket, clears a space among the mountains of papers on the table, leans over the glass surface, and starts writing while he says, "I've been thinking of sending you home in a little while. But there's a problem," and shows the magistrate the scrap of paper which reads: "Do you want to see your wife?" The magistrate nods yes while of course he's thinking no, he has no desire *to go home*, which, in Arcangelo's language, means getting to his room (windowless, no door, with surveillance and a convex mirror, same as here) in another barracks full of *carabinieri*, but of course, yes, his eyes tell Arcangelo, he wants to see his wife, no question: he hasn't seen his wife for twenty-seven days, hasn't spoken to her on the phone in five. He gestures to his watch, asking when, and says, "I've been trying to get a little sleep before finishing up a few things. I'll need at least an hour, maybe two, two and a half," while Arcangelo has written beneath his question, "Ten minutes. Stay put," which he shows the magistrate and says: "Okay. But I don't know if I can get you out of here in two hours. You might wind up waiting a little longer," and he's already standing up, putting the note back in his pocket, pencil too, already walking out of the room, winking from the doorway, smiling, as if this were all a joke. Something pops into the magistrate's head: how much this reminds him of the expression on his college classmate's face when this classmate made him come along on an errand delivering notes to another classmate, a girl from a nice home. In this nice home, they certainly couldn't turn down an espresso, but before the coffee even arrived in the small sitting room, this friend suddenly remembered another engagement, an obvious lie, and so he left him there with this girl who accepted the situation with such natural ease, she was clearly prepared for this all along, if not the one who orchestrated it in the first place. In the doorway, before he bolted, his classmate tried to give him a meaningful wink and a cheerful smile, but the smile was twisted with embarrassment.

Arcangelo has the exact same expression, the magistrate thinks, except Arcangelo is in charge of all the guardian angels so he's not the least embarrassed; his is more of an approving smile, like a teacher smiling at his clever student. Even Arcangelo admitted once that they didn't need all these precautions inside the compound, though that could change ("for now, sure, but who knows about tomorrow . . ."); still, he insisted—and the magistrate thought this was ridiculous— that they should at least follow protocol "purely as an exercise" when it came to discussing transfers: say one thing, write down another. Alone, the magistrate thinks, Funny: this time, he actually talked about a transfer, so he made a mistake, unless . . . unless someone's really listening in today, and that someone's so close, so ready to interfere, it's not enough just to keep him from knowing what we're going to do—we need to try and make him believe we're doing something else. Or maybe Arcangelo's compulsion makes him keep inventing and lying, inventing lies that keep getting riskier, closer to the truth: there have been times when the magistrate has thought that Arcangelo himself longed to be in the dark about these complicated plans that he ceaselessly worked out, modified, transformed, and, in the end, nearly always canceled.

The magistrate, stretched out in his chair once more, wonders if he's really going to see his wife tonight. It's five-fifteen. Maybe Arcangelo is playing a trick on him so he'll be more prepared, more obedient, when the actual time comes to leave. He hasn't done this yet, but he might. The last time the magistrate saw his wife, he and Arcangelo wound up in a ferocious argument. They'd dropped the magistrate off at eleven o'clock at night, in a makeshift bedroom in a *carabinieri* barracks in another city: it must have been some kind of conference room with all the furniture pushed to one side, and at the center of the room stood two little folding cots, which, if you shifted around too much, folded up on their own; his wife had been waiting there since morning, no one told her when he'd come; you have till six, Arcangelo said, practically tossing him into the room. The next day, Arcangelo defended himself, saying he didn't have a choice, her security was even more complicated than his; and the magistrate, shocked he could be so vulgar, had screamed that if Arcangelo thought all he wanted to do was fuck, then why not just bring him some train-station whore and then, for security purposes, take her and all his little notes and stuff them in the incinerator, or maybe he'd like to have a go at her himself, to blow off some steam; and Arcangelo answered in a very flat voice that if the magistrate wanted, this could be arranged, as if his screaming were really a request Arcangelo was ready to fill, within the limits of what was possible, and of course taking into account all the planning involved. Stupid idiot. But in the meantime, with Arcangelo not fighting back, the magistrate could feel his fury waning, and quit talking. I should have said something else entirely, the magistrate thinks as he sits in his chair: I should have told him how much we love each other, Renna and I, so much, that physical intimacy hardly matters anymore, all we need is a little time together, time to settle in and be tender with each other and whisper together. Probably the most beautiful thing tonight for Renna would be if she could make us supper, just a little something, and we could eat her meal together: like a married couple living in the same house, a stupid little married couple in a romance novel, the man coming home from working all day, the woman seducing him every night with her little gastronomic wonders, and of course she'll insist he stuff himself, because they don't have any children, and so he'll have to eat enough for the four children she dreams of . . .

The magistrate feels a little stupid thinking this way, but he can't help himself. Arcangelo's news (put in the form of a question, but that was really a trick: the only response to one of Arcangelo's requests was yes) has reawakened all his longing for his wife; all his longing not to be here, in these armored quarters; his longing to be another person in another world with another job. It's been four years since the magistrate realized he no longer had a choice. As soon as they relaxed his security, he'd be killed. Even if he wanted to abandon everything, the inquest, his profession, even if he went into hiding, with Renna, without Renna, someplace faraway, they'd be found and killed in no time. On the desk, four files lie open, four different testimonies about a meeting that took place in a secret mountain cabin a few months back, a meeting of representatives from the families who control people's lands, lives, and deaths; the goal of the meeting: an agreement on how to allocate each family's sphere of influence as tied to its economic and military strength, to reduce costly border wars and power struggles; an obviously provisional, illusory agreement, and certainly no peace treaty, that's come about at the request of a few families currently in a bit of trouble: these four testimonies, from people accused of various crimes who've decided to provide state's evidence, corroborate one another, corroborate so completely, that the magistrate thinks it's simply not possible they weren't carefully prepared to confuse the inquest. The magistrate knows there's always a precise correlation between a lie and the reality hidden behind that lie (Arcangelo also knows this, toys with this), and these days, his job consists of imagining, through deduction, experience, intuition, and even through pure fantasy, what the reality is that's been so carefully hidden behind these blatantly similar testimonies. Of course the witnesses themselves don't know—you'd have to be crazy to let people give false testimonies who actually had any real information: they'd let something slip and not even know it, maybe their lies would be too perfect, false truths too meticulously hiding real truths (that's what makes Arcangelo's perfectionism so costly and dangerous). While it was tough getting a hold of these people and convincing them to talk, that's still no guarantee their information's valid. They were probably already in jail when they learned what to say in their testimonies: even from jail, they could still serve the organization, could still earn their pay and protection. One of these four witness-defendants was killed in prison by a convict from an opposing family. But that doesn't mean anything, either. No security system's perfect; no one's to be completely trusted.

It's been a long while since the magistrate first realized all he felt toward the State was hatred. This wasn't the case when the inquest began. The work made him happy, a strange happiness, almost bordering on shame. His work was like that of a surgeon sinking his scalpel into flesh: the flesh was the people in these cities far from the city he called home; it was the buildings and walls here, especially in the historical districts and in the towns furthest from the cities, up in the mountains, where the forms and colors were almost Asian, gorgeous, awe-inspiring, so ancient; it was the strange countryside, arid, stubbornly cultivated, almost treeless, run through with dry, phantom-river beds that came alive only a few days a year, where, now and then while you traveled, you saw the evidence of lost prosperity, clusters of white, deserted houses; it was all of this, the flesh he cut into, and back then, so long ago, the magistrate had fooled himself into thinking he was like an expert surgeon who cuts away a tumor, who makes organs function again and restores the body to good health. That this was all false hope, foolish ambition, the magistrate only realized over time: you couldn't tell the healthy parts from those turned monstrous; blood and poison circulated in the same veins; snakes formed in women's wombs; babies hatched from snakes' eggs. It was too hard, this land, for men to live as men; maybe this wasn't always true, but by now, in this century, it was, and the magistrate felt like a torturer, like a surgeon who has before him Siamese twins that share a single heart and liver and has to pick which one to kill and which one to save. The magistrate studied the tumor, how it metastasized and spread inward from the marginal lands where it exerted its control toward the center, creeping into the capital like the hyphae of some fungus; and then there was that terrible time he'd never forget, in a sumptuous ministry office, and what he saw in his superior's face, his superior who was complimenting him in such noble, generic language, commending him for his work so far, urging him to continue with the inquest, and this was the exact reason, his superior announced—so the inquest could be even more fruitful—that some areas of the inquest were being removed from his jurisdiction and assigned to other magistrates, for maximized effort, and the magistrate saw in his superior's face, he recognized, the all too present signs of evil. Oh, of course this high official, so dignified, so pompous, wasn't controlled by one of the families, and if the magistrate had told this official what he'd seen in his face, the man would have been outraged, would have screamed, his face turning red (and the tumor, more obvious), and kicked the magistrate out of his office and run to a higher official demanding the impudent magistrate's head. No, it certainly wasn't one of the families that controlled this official: it was a thousand reckless instincts that always kept him wanting more, though never the one thing truly worth wanting—the destruction of the families. Rather than letting himself obsess over that, like a doctor lets himself obsess over someone ill, this high official simply let himself be distracted: maybe he wanted a position for someone close to him, or for someone close to someone close to him, and the inquest might help that person's reputation, help launch a career or provide a noble finish to one that was otherwise drab; maybe with this inquest, he wanted to apply good common sense (one person doing the work vs. more people doing more and even better work), which he still wanted to believe in, even if the families' increased power these last few years had torn the State apart; maybe he wanted to satisfy someone he felt obliged to—for noble reasons, of course. The magistrate hadn't told this high official what he read in his face because he didn't want to be cut off from everything: that would have compromised the inquest completely.

That was the first compromise: the magistrate decided to live with the tumor because cutting into it in any one place would mean losing the chance to cut into it. For a while, the magistrate considered this compromise *playing it smart*; but before too long, he knew he hadn't so much played as lost. Then one day he realized that through this loss, the tumor had now spread to him: in a way, he continued with the inquest because the families let him, but only with those parts of the inquest that they hadn't taken away, or rather, with those parts of the inquest that they let him continue with. He couldn't help thinking that the families must profit from the inquest, though in some secret way impossible to tell: the magistrate already knew that sometimes the stronger families left it to state law to liquidate the smaller families; first, though, they'd make sure and kill the bosses and anyone else who might know something important or that couldn't be recycled once he was cleaned up and gotten under control; then they'd leak something small and let *the law* scrape off the plate.

The magistrate only met one family member who decided to tell the actual truth. This was an important man in his family, and he'd turned over some valuable information. He was nothing like the four fake witnesses whose four files lay open on the magistrate's table, or any of the other dozens of fake witnesses the magistrate had encountered over his years on the inquest. When the *carabinieri* raided his hideout, this man was holding a submachine gun, and he shot and killed two young officers. At his trial, he was convicted only for this, along with possession of a military weapon; the court couldn't be convinced of this man's high position in his criminal family. He sat in his cell for almost two years without saying a word. Then he asked to speak to the magistrate, and slowly, he forced the words out, they seemed to stick in his throat, to be anchored behind his teeth, and he'd stop himself to cry, trembling, never looking up, wringing his hands, whispering, barely audible, as he gave out detail after detail, later all confirmed: people's names, the organization's decision-making process, bank accounts, addresses, future plans. The first interview lasted six hours, from ten in the morning until four in the afternoon, then the man collapsed from exhaustion; afterward, the magistrate's first thought was for the safety of the man's family, his elderly mother and his wife; he managed to keep them alive for almost two weeks and got them the man's brief note just in time, which basically said: I killed you, forgive me, I don't want to see you. Miraculously, the man stayed alive another three years, and some of the inquest's definitive cases were brought to a close thanks to him; that this so-called *key witness* survived so long was clear proof for the defense that his testimony wasn't reliable.

The magistrate felt oddly disturbed by this key witness. He felt an odd love, an empathy toward this man. He'd never have believed it if the man said he'd decided to talk because, over two years of isolation and silence, he'd come to recognize justice; but the key witness never said anything of the kind. He was elliptic concerning these matters, a strange contrast to his hesitant yet precise description of events that occurred. One day, responding to one of the magistrate's questions, the key witness said: "You, Mr. Prosecutor, they're going to kill. No matter how well you're protected. You don't know when, but you already know there's no escape. You already know there's no escape, but you don't know when. And there's no getting out of it: the longer the inquest goes, the uglier your death will be. But somewhere down the line, you can choose a day to die. All you have to do, the day you're ready, is step outside in your shirtsleeves and go for a gelato in the piazza."

This is what the key witness said. Less than two weeks before, during a night of tears, the magistrate and Renna, who was unexpectedly pregnant, had decided she'd have an abortion. That night they realized they couldn't bring someone into this world. It wasn't just the unlikelihood, so painfully obvious, that this child would ever see his parents grow old or that he himself would ever reach adolescence or young adulthood. It was also, above all, their complete lack of hope in any future. By now, the magistrate and his wife didn't find life worth living without their moments, their fragments of happiness found only on occasion in the present. They wouldn't know what to give a child; they'd raise him like a plant blowing in the wind. And so they decided she'd have an abortion, no matter how repugnant the idea. Their decision felt supremely unjust, but they didn't know what they could decide that was less unjust. In the years that followed, their child showed up often in their dreams: he was a boy with bright eyes touched with gray, light blond hair, thin lips, extremely small hands, disproportionately small, like a doll's. He was always wearing jeans and a red shirt. In their dreams, the child was with his parents in a big field of dark grass, the woods off in the distance, no clouds in the sky but also no sun, a sky filled with silver light. They were strolling in the field, and then the son walked off toward the woods, looking back now and then at his parents who couldn't follow. He didn't seem to hate them for killing him, and that was a comfort. But his red shirt was blood-red, and that was painful.

The magistrate had only a short time to get the most dangerous papers into the safe.

He slipped them into their files, opened the safe, put the files inside, closed the safe, went back to the table and started flipping through an enormous *ABI* volume, the proceedings of a conference of the Italian Banking Association on money laundering. If someone was listening in, he needed to think the magistrate was still working, that he'd set some documents aside for something else. The magistrate had once tried getting an arrest warrant for a participant of this conference, one of the chairmen who'd proposed what was probably the most astute, impregnable set of controls. Of course there wasn't much evidence, just some testimony in exchange for a deal, so not very credible; still, the magistrate recognized the same intellectual style in some of the laundering operations that he saw in this set of controls (never actually applied) from the report. These were the words he let slip, *intellectual style*, and they laughed in his face. "Now you're seeing ghosts," they snorted.

"Next you'll want us to arrest the Interior Minister because he walks like a criminal, or the Pope because, from behind, he's got the neck of a felon. You've got a case of Lombrosian prejudice, you know—you're inventing an intellectual physiognomy—you want to arrest people based on the quality of their souls. Oh, please do go on with the inquest—we're not here to protect anyone—if you want to arrest a bank president, we're certainly not going to stop you, but you need to learn how to tell the difference between motives for arrest and oracles. You're identifying far too much with your work: you have to remember, it's not your job to institute justice throughout the land. All those who dreamed of bringing back a paradise on earth just wound up producing indiscriminate terror—if we left it up to you, you'd arrest anyone in this wretched country who had the slightest bit of power." And so the bank president remained safe and clear at the helm of his bank, although maybe he didn't feel quite so safe now that (for reasons the magistrate hoped stayed a mystery) certain channels had been, if not cut off, at least restricted, and certain contacts had grown weaker, certain people less reliable.

With the secret complicity of one of the bank executives, a subordinate to the president though still fairly autonomous, the magistrate got some people transferred from one branch to another; had the duties changed for others; even managed to corrupt someone and turn him into an informant. If the flow of money were slowed down or interrupted, he might just be able to use this as evidence, and *evidence to the contrary*, that the bank president was guilty; at least it might cause a few problems, force those making use of the money to change their procedures or commit some kind of error.

Arcangelo had said ten minutes, but all that meant was: "No advance warning." One of the guardian angels paused in the doorway, glanced to the empty side of the room, to the mirror, then glanced at the magistrate by his desk and smiled.

Just kids, twenty-two to twenty-four years old, all handpicked by Arcangelo: in a way, they revered the magistrate; they treated him with the respect you might hold for an ancient relic, a precious Chinese vase, but it was Arcangelo they obeyed, down to the smallest detail. The boy disappeared from the mirror; the magistrate heard his

light step a few seconds more. One day, when yet another trial ended
without a conviction due to contradictory testimony and problems
interpreting the evidence (even though everyone knew, in their heart
of hearts, that the accused were guilty), the magistrate had sent a top-
secret letter to the capital, which basically said: I can't take it anymore, I'm worn out, my brain's not working anymore; a few days later,
the head of state himself called to say that the State really couldn't
manage without him; his experience was indispensable, his devotion,
most admirable and meritorious; and for everything he'd done and
might do in the future, he'd have the eternal gratitude of an entire
nation; and he was wrong to feel isolated and abandoned, even if the
head of state understood his frame of mind, down there, so close to
the capital, maybe two-hundred kilometers' distance, but light years
away; and then a few days after that, Arcangelo showed up with his
black suit and black hair, and he handed the magistrate a letter (the
signature looked a great deal like the Interior Minister's) and told
him: "I'm here for your security. You can accept or refuse my services.
If you accept, then you have to accept whatever measures I take, and
if you refuse, then I've been instructed to inform you we can't be held
responsible for your security"; and the magistrate consented; there
was nothing left to do: he could either choose to die soon, by the *gela-
teria* in the piazza, or he could die a little later, though he'd certainly
still die, and this wasn't too far off, either, maybe at the hands of this
very man who didn't seem to have a real name, and so the magistrate
dubbed him Arcangelo.

He didn't take Arcangelo on because he had any hope for the
future. He wasn't afraid, either (though they apparently thought he
was, since they sent him Arcangelo). Still, once he understood that by
sending Arcangelo, they'd washed their hands of his fate, the magistrate decided to survive. From then on, after Arcangelo arrived, he'd
pretty much done what Arcangelo wanted, meaning his security—or

more accurately, his survival—was Arcangelo's problem now; he'd stop struggling to survive; Arcangelo struggled for him; the magistrate focused on going ahead with the inquest, working as hard as he could, because he knew as long as there was an inquest, he'd have Arcangelo, and that there'd be an inquest forever, because as soon as you cut off one branch, two more grew back; it wasn't like it once was, in years past: he no longer did this out of any sense of justice, or because he hated these ferocious criminal families, these drug dealers, gunrunners, racketeers, these criminals in their white gloves, secret bosses but public officials in local administrations—by now, he did all this out of love for Renna, to have one day more, to be able to hold her now and then, to cry with her and collect her tears, to vindicate the death of their child with love, a love composed almost entirely of distant thoughts, of controlled phone calls, of sudden, guarded meetings, with no intimacy whatsoever, no surprises, no relations, no hope.

Once, the magistrate, not even knowing why, suddenly asked Arcangelo—"And what about you—do you have a wife somewhere?"—and to his surprise, Arcangelo reached into his inside jacket pocket and pulled out a leather case with a photo of a plain, chubby girl in a bathing suit, a blond, naked baby in her arms, some unknown body of water behind her, her mouth strained, eyes narrowed against the sun, blond hair barely held back, stringy and tangled around her face. Another photo showed this same girl, thinner, prettier, in jeans and blue canvas shoes, in a white blouse that tied in the front, very Seventies style, her mouth and eyes laughing, practically climbing onto the pedestal of an awful gilded statue, and there in the background was the Eiffel Tower, of course. "How long since you've seen her?" the magistrate whispered, still stunned, and Arcangelo didn't answer, just tucked the case away, and squinted at the magistrate, like someone who'd been extorted, tricked into sharing a confidence he really didn't want to share. But the magistrate understood this lesson, and

the next day he asked that one of the guardian angels be sent to his
real house for a box of photographs he had in a drawer; he found the
photo he was looking for, a very old black and white snapshot from
when they'd only known each other a few weeks, taken in a photo
booth in the Bologna train station, that time they'd gone to the Patti
Smith concert and missed the last train, and so they had to wait for
two hours in the middle of the night, almost till morning; at first they
wandered around the dark, deserted city, then exhausted, they sought
refuge in the station, but there were already bums on all the benches
and steps, and in the photo booth, they took that passport-sized photo
of the two of them that looked a bit distorted; the taxi drivers outside
the station offered them some wine, they were so hungry and tired
and dazed: Renna had a big nose and thick lips, her most beautiful
feature, and he still had that beard covering his baby face, his best
feature, Renna taught him later, but at that point he was so timid and
embarrassed, he tried to hide it. The photograph fit in his wallet, it
would be a little creased, but that didn't matter: it didn't have to last
very long. That night, many hours later, the train arrived, headed
from Vienna to Rome, and there were only berths, so theoretically,
they weren't allowed on, but the kind conductor told them, "Climb
up," and "Watch your step," and in the berth of an empty compartment they dropped off to sleep, on top of each other, and that was
their extremely innocent first night together; they woke up almost to
Rome and began giving each other tiny kisses and caresses, dazed and
happy, stinky and dreamy.

Renna looked very small, sitting with her heels tucked under her
in the backseat of the enormous car, her shoes kicked off, wearing a
worn-out blue linen suit; she was thin, her face drawn, dark, her nose
huge now, her lips extremely thin; she only said, "Hi," as the guardian angels hurled him inside, and he took her right hand in his left,
her hand felt light and fragile, and he clutched it and didn't let go.

Arcangelo got in up front beside the driver. The motorcade sped off, who knows where they were taking them, there had to be at least two cars ahead and two cars behind, sirens screaming; they were out of the city almost at once, then onto the highway, not stopping, through the public-vehicle tollbooth, speeding along as fast as possible, they're taking us to the airport, the magistrate thought, then he thought how strange, Arcangelo never goes in my car, then he felt the impact and Arcangelo was rising up, arms open, head back, almost on top of him; and he felt the car flying, metal opening below his feet, crumpling, red hot, burning, devouring Renna's legs; he heard Renna screaming and felt the pressure crushing his chest, pushing his eyes into his head, throwing his head back; he felt something that wasn't flesh inside his flesh, cutting, separating his chest from his belly, his right arm from his torso; and with all his remaining strength, the magistrate gripped Renna's hand, and as long as he was able to love her he loved her.

## Translator's Acknowledgements

I wish to thank John Behling, John DuVal, Louise Rozier, and Kaija Straumanis for their careful readings of these stories and for their invaluable feedback. I am also grateful to the University of North Dakota for providing me with the much-needed time and funding to finish the translations of these stories. Thank you to Marco Candida and to my parents. Most of all, I wish to thank Giulio Mozzi for his patience in answering my many questions and for his beautiful stories.

## Translator's Note

English-language readers might miss the following:
-Yanez, the main character in "Claw," is the same Yanez who is the "sidekick" of the pirate, Sandokan, from a famous series of adventure novels by the nineteenth-century Italian writer Emilio Salgari.
-The word "tana" (from the story "Tana"), means "burrow" in Italian.

Giulio Mozzi has published more than twenty-five books—as a fiction writer, poet, and editor. He is primarily known for his story collections, especially *This Is the Garden*, which won the Premio Mondello. "The Apprentice" (included in this collection) appears in an anthology of the top Italian stories of the twentieth century. He has even created an imaginary artist, Carlo Dalcielo, whose work has appeared in public exhibitions and books, like Dalkey Archive Press's *Best European Fiction 2010*.

Elizabeth Harris's translations have appeared in anthologies and numerous journals. She is also the translator of Mario Rigoni Stern's *Giacomo's Seasons* (Autumn Hill Books) and Antonio Tabucchi's *Tristano Dies* (Archipelago Books), for which she received a 2013 PEN/Heim Translation Fund grant. She teaches creative writing at the University of North Dakota.

Open Letter—the University of Rochester's nonprofit, literary translation press—is one of only a handful of publishing houses dedicated to increasing access to world literature for English readers. Publishing ten titles in translation each year, Open Letter searches for works that are extraordinary and influential, works that we hope will become the classics of tomorrow.

Making world literature available in English is crucial to opening our cultural borders, and its availability plays a vital role in maintaining a healthy and vibrant book culture. Open Letter strives to cultivate an audience for these works by helping readers discover imaginative, stunning works of fiction and poetry, and by creating a constellation of international writing that is engaging, stimulating, and enduring.

Current and forthcoming titles from Open Letter include works from Argentina, Bulgaria, Denmark, France, Germany, Latvia, Poland, Russia, and many other countries.

www.openletterbooks.org